The Joyful Revolution

A future history of the State of Jefferson

By Glenn Melosh

Cover art by Celeste Melosh

Edited by Vicki "Comma Bomber" Suemnicht

Contributions from Tricia Melosh

Copyright 2024

Dedicated to The Light of My Life

Preface

Joy and invention have the power to inspire a revolution that changes the world, without resorting to violence. For examples consider the Renaissance or the Summer of Love.

Inspiration for The Joyful Revolution struck while I was rowing a raft through high water on the Carson River with a bunch of hairy river rats. By hairy, I mean we were all clearly mammals, apparently from a human subspecies. These types all tell stories. Some are mostly true, some are funny, and others rhyme.

I was pulling off a vicious rock bank on river right when the tall commanding figure of a woman appeared on the shore in magenta and black whitewater gear and beckoned to us. I pulled into the next eddy. Who was she? Then there she was again, helping pull out an elaborate lunch on a sandy beach under shady pines along with the rest of our tribe. It seemed that she was one of us, or vice versa.

As we sat in the sand on that sparkling early summer day, she told a story about the Eel River and how a diversion tunnel was sending its life blood to a river to the south to feed reservoirs and vineyards. Sounding aggrieved, she asked how could we stop this water theft. Her anguish inspired me to offer an answer that spun out of control and formed this story.

Meanwhile, it also changed my life. We now live part time on the Eel River. Moving to Mendocino County resulted in meeting a lot of eccentric people. This book is a testament to their stories and their tolerance for each other.

Almost all the characters in this book are made up. I took some liberties with stories people told me by pasting them on to these cartoonish figures. I hope the original story-tellers can forgive me. (On the other hand, I am not sorry.)

If one of these stolen stories is yours, you might wonder, have I no shame? My responses are: 1. Yes, I have no shame and 2. Once you tell a story, it has a life of its' own, so you shouldn't be surprised about the company it keeps.

Bruce Anderson, the only real person in the book and the editor of the Anderson Valley Advertiser (AVA), said "You can invoke my name any way you want." He turns out to be a hero in the book, which may also be true in real life. But who am I to judge? The articles from the AVA in the story are completely made up and have not been published in the newspaper, yet.

Finally, I want to thank the right-wing acolytes of the past history of the State of Jefferson. They are keeping the dream alive. This dream may yet soar, but as Ryder Jeffers recognizes, it takes two wings to fly.

1

Before the Future

I grew up pushing dusty herds of cattle back and forth along the concrete sidewalk on the suburban street in front of my house in South Chicago. I lived a dream in bright colors, until my dream was ripped away from me and I got run off the range by a rogue federal agent. I only got back to driving cattle during the revolution.

My name is Ryder. My name felt cool when I was young because I could see myself riding on my palomino, pushing them longhorns across the prairie, waving my broad-brimmed hat, whooping, and beating the dust off my jeans. Then I would stretch up my lean body, slap my hat back on my sweat-streaked head, and ride down a stray doggie thundering along on my trusty horse. "Yeehaw!" I looked great in the mirror. I was living a boyhood American dream and it felt good.

My parents indulged me by springing for riding lessons, horse camp, and a cowboy hat with a shiny plastic star. I found a holster and cap guns under the Christmas tree and put cowboy posters up in my room. I even started walking around a little bow-legged because of the way it made me feel. Try it sometime, it feels studly.

When I was about ten, I would play in my backyard roping a fence post with an old clothesline as a lasso. I would sing the TV theme to Bonanza while throwing, then recoiling my rope.

One bright Saturday morning, while I was perfecting my loop work, the girl next door looked over the fence and asked what was going on. She had dark eyes and straight dark hair. Her skin was pale but pink in the sun. I told her what I was doing and she said, "Cool," then asked if she could play and came over.

She bounced in through the gate wearing pedal-pushers and Converse high-tops. She sang out her name, "I'm Anna Bobana" and added "Fee Fi Fo Fana" from the song, The Name Game. After she tried looping the post a few times, she had the idea to nail corn cobs to the post as horns. "Now it's real," she said. Anna was a couple of years older than me and mostly better at stuff, but we had a great time whooping and looping that post.

Then we had the idea to try some trick-riding on our bikes. We spent time practicing over the next few months and got so we could roll pretty fancy. We yelled, "git-up" and "move it" while driving an imaginary herd of cattle along our dusty concrete trail. She was faster but I showed her how to stand up on the cross-bar of her bike on one foot while leaning over to steer.

Once I asked her why she hung out with me. She said, "Oh, those older boys are no fun." I wasn't sure what that meant.

One day, I convinced Anna that we should head over to the next block on a cattle drive. I said, "Cattle drives used to come into Chicago all the time. We need to get our cattle to market."

We rounded up the herd and got 'em moving. As we were coming around the corner into the next neighborhood, pushing imaginary cattle and a cloud of dust, we saw some older boys cruising along on bikes. A couple of them had their t-shirt sleeves ripped off like they thought they were tough. They saw us and one of them yelled, "Hey, it's that girl from school. Let's get her!"

They immediately started peddling fast, trying to cut us off. I was behind and without thinking, I sped up, pumping like crazy. I sang the notes of the theme to the Lone Ranger as I accelerated. For once I was catching up with Anna. I sliced my bike between her and them, just like we had practiced when cutting out imaginary calves from the herd. Those boys had to turn or crash. They skidded on the asphalt and shouted, "Hey, jerk face!" Then ahead, Anna found a gap in the parked cars, swerved through, jumped the curb, thumped onto the sidewalk, and was long gone.

They got back up on their bikes and went after her. I knew they couldn't catch her now and quietly turned back to my house, my bike tires humming. I felt fierce.

I dismounted in front of my house and swaggered a bit while rolling my bike into the garage.

The next day after school, Anna came over and thanked me, smiled serenely, and gave me a light kiss on the cheek. I flushed warm and buzzy inside. It was a moment I can still feel.

The next two months were glorious, but then one day she told me she was moving to Orlando. I said, "Don't… Is that in Indiana?" and "Why?" She pointed out that the boys from the next block had been hassling her at school. Her parents said that they didn't need to put up with that. They had family in Orlando.

She moved and I felt abandoned, but it seemed like it was my fault. I never should have made her go with me on that cattle drive.

I still had my dream, but it felt lonely and my dreamland started fading into the sunset.

Then one afternoon in sixth grade, my mom sat me down in the kitchen saying, "We gotta talk." I remember the scuffed yellow and tan linoleum on the floor and the grey light from the cloudy sky coming in the window. Those wood chairs were never comfortable and always squeaky. She looked as serious as an unpaid bill with her thin dark hair and worry lines. The light made her seem dim.

I thought it was going to be the birds and bees, but instead she said, "You can't wear that little kid cowboy hat anymore. You just look stupid."

Then she told me how my name really came from the side of a double-parked Ryder rental truck that blocked the road to the hospital while I was being born in the back seat of a beat-up Geo Metro. I was staggered. "You mean I'm named after a moving truck?"

She said, "And you aren't cut out to be a cowboy. You're not lanky; you're just skinny and cowboys don't wear glasses. If you wear that stupid cowboy hat, people are gonna laugh." She continued, "They don't pay people to ride horses anymore so you should start thinking about business or accounting or something. You don't want to end up like your dad."

"Just be normal," she said. "It's not exciting, but it works."

I tried to put her off by suggesting that instead of a cowboy, maybe I could be a forester or a fishing guide. My mind was reeling, just trying to fend off her caustic dismissal. Deep down I knew that being a cowboy wasn't going to happen, but I didn't want to hear about it.

My bright vision of the future that I had carefully protected from reality flapped like an old paper poster for Buffalo Bill's Wild West Show stapled to a telephone pole in the gusty wind off Lake Michigan. I had been happily dazzled by imaginary bright lights and the thought of "real Indians" until she lifted the canvas to show the hairy ankles of grubby roustabouts paid minimum wage to sustain the illusion.

She looked at me with disappointed eyes and laid down what she called the bitter truth. "Your dad has a lot of dreams too, but they never work out, so give it up and get yourself a real life." I didn't like the taste of that.

As the year wore on, her persistent snark about my failed dreams left me with lot of self-doubt and confusion. She probably just wanted me to get on with my life. Unfortunately, she was articulate in addition to being cynical. I was still young and I hadn't built my confidence, so I couldn't protect my fragile dreams with snappy comebacks.

In contrast, my dad was a schemer, a story-teller, and a con artist. He would work one job full of enthusiasm, then disappointed, he would leave (meaning he got fired) and start another. He had a great voice and wavy black hair. Finally, after getting fired again, he went out on his own, first selling shoes door to door, then vegetables, and eventually, real estate.

Even when I was in middle school, he would enlist my help. In high school he bought me a used pick-up truck so I could deliver newspapers and the "organic, farm-fresh vegetables" that he was selling by subscription. That truck was a "beater," so beat up already that it didn't matter what happened to it next. He told me not to bother with a driver's license until later.

One day my dad asked me to help pick up some vegetables with him at the Savemart. I drove over looking at people on the street and wondering what their lives were like. What is a normal life? I asked myself.

Then I parked behind the store to meet him near the dumpsters. There was a big pile of empty cardboard boxes and wood vegetable crates against the wall. I stepped out of my pickup truck to the overripe smells of discarded fruit. The black pavement felt sticky as I walked to the back of the store. The base of the back wall was slashed with graffiti.

After a few moments, my dad came through the door carrying bags full of vegetables. He had bought them on sale. He was happy, as usual, and greeted me with "You won't believe the price I got on these veggies. And they have enough flaws on them to look organic."

I was secretly relieved that he hadn't climbed out of one of the dumpsters.

We repacked the vegetables in discarded wood produce crates from the pile. Then he sent me to deliver them. I drove my pickup around on his route and dropped off crates to people. He tucked some straw into my shoe laces for effect and told me to say "farm fresh" when I dropped them off.

That worked for a while, but he was still short of money. So, he decided to go big time and that meant real estate.

He got the idea to sell "Grade AA" land in Hawaii. This sounded attractive to anyone living in Chicago in the winter, even me, especially when he showed them stunning photos of the blue Pacific Ocean in the sun over a slim horizon of black land. He would say, in a deep tone, "Land that color must have rich soil."

He didn't tell people that the "AA" referred to a type of sharp fragmental lava that was not only nearly unusable and dangerous to walk on, but faced a serious risk of being covered by new lava. I think the Hawaiians call the lava "AA" because of how they cry out when crossing the lava in bare feet. Also, any soil that might develop on these fresh rocky fields could be rich but was still hundreds of years in the future.

Of course, I loved him and his dreams. And who was I to question his tactics. I had enough trouble just surviving 10th grade. His world seemed so much better than mine.

Finally, he opened his own bank to make the loans for his Hawaiian land deals. Other banks were balking, even though he supplied them with top-quality documents adorned with flourishing signatures that he bought downtown somewhere. He opened his own office in a recently closed bank building, so it looked right and still had a vault. He hired a teller to accept deposits (mom refused to participate) and a very nice-looking loan officer to close the deals. Then he bundled the loans and sold them on the securities market. Everybody got worthless paper and he was finally flush with cash.

He benefited even more directly from the bank by borrowing depositor cash back from his own bank only to declare bankruptcy later. He would happily stamp his own loan documents with a big hand stamp that said, "Bad Debt," while saying to himself, "This jerk will never pay us back."

He advertised his bank as a member of the FTIC. Nobody checked on what that meant. It seemed to me later that instead of the Federal Deposit Insurance Corp. it must have stood for "Fast-Talking Investment Con."

Meanwhile, his real estate scheme got out of hand after a while because it was popular and people heard about it. Once the word spread, he started getting competitive bidders showing up in his office. People wanted in on the deal. He couldn't accommodate them all, so there were a few disgruntled potential buyers. Somebody must have talked.

2

Childhood's End

I am in a meeting room at the High Hat Hotel watching my dad work his investors. He stands on an elevated platform, with his wavy hair and deep voice. He is walking back and forth while waving his hands painting a romantic word picture of the region in Hawaii and the development plans that he wants them to fund for their properties. The furnishings in the room are folding chairs full of people and a podium to one side of the platform. All the colors are hotel bland. There is a faint smell of old carpet.

As he finishes with "This is the real deal," four men in dark suits, long coats, and short haircuts stand up from the audience. Three of them step so their backs are to the wall and one walks to the podium. Another man steps inside and stands blocking the door. He wears black tactical gear and carries an assault rifle across his chest.

The new man at the podium says, "I am FBI Special Agent Fred Arally. This man, Tom Jeffers, is under arrest for securities fraud and tax evasion. You are all material witnesses and will need to make statements." He glares at the audience with an intimidating look that he must have practiced in special agent school. He looks at each one in the audience to ensure compliance.

The audience is shocked and, after a moment, an audible rumble is heard. Then, one of them cries out, "Hey, what about our money?"

Three more people in suits enter the room as if on cue. Two are carrying folding tables and another struts in behind them. The first two set up the tables and pull over some folding chairs.

The third man is wearing a well-cut grey shark suit and slick hair, Chicago style. He announces, "I am Marc Aguila, Esquire. We will be forming a class action suit for asset recovery. Those of you interested in getting back some of your investment, feel free to sign up with my associates," he says, gesturing at the tables.

"I will only get paid my standard legal fees when you get paid," he says.

"How much are the fees?" asks someone from the audience.

"In these cases, the traditional standard fees come from the received assets and amount to a judicially-approved portion of the gross," says Mr. Aguila.

"How much?"

In a lower voice, he mumbles, "Fees are assessed at 40% plus expenses." Then he quickly claps loudly, twice.

Immediately two waitresses burst into the room wearing short black skirts and white dress shirts with black bow ties. They sashay up the aisle carrying trays of snacks and drinks. An aroma of donuts and black coffee wafts over the room as the ladies set down the trays and spin to the crowd in unison, gesturing to the food between them.

"While you are waiting," announces the lawyer, "please relax and enjoy some refreshments… Consider this an early return on your participation."

As the audience crowds around the donuts, my dad is getting handcuffed by two FBI agents. The agents bunch around him and follow Special Agent Arally out of the room almost marching, with their shiny black shoes stomping the floor. The armed guard faces the room once more and then closes the door upon leaving.

I am shocked and still in my seat, wondering what just happened. I am even more upset because my dad's schemes always seemed a little off to me, but I hadn't questioned them. He is my dad, so I had somehow suspended disbelief despite what I witnessed. I should have asked him to dial it back or just get a real job, instead I helped.

It never happens like this in any of the sit-coms I am watching.

3

The Sky is Cloudy All Day

I am still a little woozy from shock when I get out of bed the next day. The dim light of morning seems odd, as if it is not the same world as yesterday. On the street it seems that nobody noticed the sun is upside down as it beams cold through the clouds.

This lasts for a couple of weeks. I climb in my pick-up truck to get to school every day. At least my truck is the same as always. It's run-down, but still working.

Two weeks later, as I drive through the drizzly black streets, depressed, I stop and go at all the usual places while my brain is on automatic. I park and walk in from the parking lot to the school through a soaking mist. My backpack weighs heavy on my back with books as I trudge through the rain.

A man in a dark suit and a buzz cut is standing on the sidewalk below the steps, near the entry to the school. I wonder what he is doing here. He raises his hand, "Are you Ryder Jeffers? My name is Special Agent

Fred Arally." He shows me a badge. "You're Tom Jeffers' son, right? He needs your help."

Then I recognize him from the arrest at the High Hat Hotel. Aggravated, I growl, "You want my help?" I look at him more closely and think, so that is what they mean by beady eyes. They are small, mean, and stick out a little, like he has been holding his breath too long.

"You can help with restitution," he says. "That means if we get the money back, your dad might get favorable treatment from the judge."

I think about this for a moment, wondering what this really means. Then I remember I am talking to the FBI and I start feeling protective. It feels deep, visceral, and involuntary. This guy is after my dad.

"Well Mr. Special Agent, it seems to me that you are just looking for more evidence," I tell him, "Plus, I don't know about any money."

His grimace makes me think he assumes that I'll roll-over for his slick, patronizing, official attitude. But hey, I already know about slick, it's just that my dad made it look good.

As I walk past him, he raises his arms so his jacket opens, showing that he is armed. He moves to block me. I say, "I have class" and step around him.

He reaches out and grabs me. He is big and stronger than I am, but something about how he holds me feels weird. Reflexively, I dig my fingers into his armpit and start tickling. He giggles and drops his arms to protect himself. I bolt. He starts coming after me, but is stopped by Dr. Osgood, the janitor.

Charles Osgood is my only true friend at the school. He is brilliant, wise, and six and a half feet of handsome black muscle. He once told me he works as a janitor because nobody in Chicago wants to hire a black physicist, even with a PhD in hydraulic engineering.

Dr. Osgood steps between us, calmly raising one hand like a traffic cop while his other carries a long handle with a floppy mop head. "You got a gun, but I got a mop. So back off."

Charles continues, "I heard you say you're with the FBI, but I am not letting you on campus without permission."

Agent Arally reaches into his coat. Charles scowls, "So now you're gonna shoot *another* black man?"

Agent Arally stops, taken aback.

"I didn't think so," Charles continues. "If you want to go on campus, you gotta go to the principal first." He points imperiously with one massive hand to the office.

Special Agent Arally looks at Charles, then gets an angry anguished look that reddens his face. He turns and walks away down the stairs and toward the parking lot. Then he starts to scuttle. Somehow Charles hit a nerve.

My janitor friend says to me, "What's he running from? My mop?"

As Charles and I watch him hurry to his vehicle, I puzzle, "What just happened?"

Charles says, "Most bullies are broken inside. You just have to push them where it hurts. He must be hurting bad."

I reply, giddy, "Oh yeah, or maybe it was your scary mop."

"Oh, do you like it?" Charles smiles. "It's quite a bit more than just a mop. I invented onboard jet nozzles with a water pump and recovery system activated by twisting the handle. I call it the Hydromopster®. It works out your forearms and hands a bit." He holds up his arms and hands and they are heavily roped with muscle.

Then he turns to me to say, "Seriously, the FBI has power and a history. If they don't like you, they can take you down one way or another. I am not saying you should cooperate, but you need to think about it."

I immediately decide that no, I am not going to think about it.

As he leaves the school, Arally chokes with regret and pain, and then anger. It wasn't me, he thinks. But the bloody scenes from shootings, with black men lying dead, haunt him. He shuts his eyes. I had to protect myself, he thinks. It was their fault. They shouldn't have moved.

4

After The Fall

Unfortunately, my recalcitrant attitude doesn't stop the Feds. After an agonizing several months full of uncertainty, my creative and convincing father pleads to tax evasion and ends up in federal prison.

I get abandoned, again. I think, was it my fault, for not speaking up? If it weren't for my dad's plea deal, I might be in jail too.

After months of agony, I drive out in my pickup to visit him at Stateville Correctional. I park my truck in a vast parking lot and walk toward the prison's wire-topped walls. The view of the guard towers and wire is depressing.

As I enter the front gate it feels official and final. I feel like I don't belong. I get scanned for weapons at security and led into the building by a guard. The guards have the smug superior attitude endemic to powerless people in power over others. I feel a little sorry for them.

We pass through long fluorescent-lit concrete hallways and multiple stage-locked double gates to a group meeting room. The place smells like industrial cleaner. The room colors are shades of grey and tan. The sky outside the high windows is also grey. The guard whispers, "Let your dad know that I have his package for him."

My dad shows up in a pressed orange prison jumpsuit and nice shoes. His skin, in contrast to the room, looks pink and his eyes are alive. His wavy dark hair is now cut prison-short but he is smiling at me. We sit down at a worn table with chairs that are bolted down and he says, "Ryder, thanks for coming."

Concerned about him being in prison I ask, "What's going on in here? You keeping busy? Are you safe?"

"Yes I'm safe and busier than ever. All the violent convicts are in other cell blocks."

"OK, but being in here must be frustrating."

Then he says, "It turns out most of the white-collar guys in here want to invest. I tell them, why let the banks reap all the profits? Those banks in Panama are all crooked. That's why they take our dirty money. Meanwhile, the more my new friends invest, the more I can skim."

I reply, "But dad, that's how you got here."

"Right, but it turns out that what I was doing was mostly legal and it's how the rich run the country… Meanwhile, I pled guilty on tax issues. They can't let those slide, otherwise how would they fund their beltway scams? Now I can make more than when I was out, I will just have to pay the government their cut somehow.”

“You could help,” he says. ”You could be an investment advisor helping me launder my clients’ money online. If we can just figure out how to pay taxes on hidden income, we will be golden.”

I look around and back at him. “I love you Dad, but not enough to move in with you.”

It feels good to be with him, but my adolescent adoration for my colorful father is cracked, like his skin is peeling back revealing patches of the pale skin of a con man. I love him, but I don’t want to be him.

In that moment, the similarity of my parent’s suggestions for my future strikes me. They’re both talking about a business career. This is confusing.

Everyone else in my school is slotting themselves into cliques: jocks, nerds, dopers, dweebs, or surfers (on lake Michigan of all places!). Each group has standards of behavior, dress, and language. They follow each other around, do the same stuff, and say the same things. But because of my father, I don’t fit. I am a “bad apple,” despite my technical innocence due to the terms of his plea deal.

The thought of a life in business or accounting sounds to me like a grown-up nerd or maybe a dweeb. Meanwhile working with hoods to cover up criminal income seems worse. One brush with a possible jail term is enough.

Back at school, my angst about being accepted or at least ignored makes me cringe when I think about my dad. I feel guilty. Meanwhile, my schoolmates are cruel as they divert attention from their own emotional struggles. They lay all their self-doubt on me and laugh about my dad, while making jokes about my future as a convict.

One day somebody puts a fart cushion on my seat in class. When I sit down, I make a loud blat. Everyone laughs, even the teacher. I feel sheepish, terrible, and guilty, but then shift to rebellious. Why should I care? They don't care about me. So, after class, when I get up from my seat, I grab that thing and put it in my back pocket. Now I can disrupt class any time I want. When I get bored, I just pump it out. This is high school so I go off pretty regular. The girls I had no chance with anyway say, "Gross" and I reply, "What?"

I am lonely through the rest of high school. I adjust by controlling my anger and keeping my mouth shut. I never volunteer in class to avoid the back comments. I just stick to bashing out my assignments as revenge. Any of my frequent adolescent boy fantasies about the girls in my school never have a chance.

Meanwhile, my mother has to deal with the same kind of disappointment about her husband and responds with a cold-hearted cynicism that seems to encompass me as well since I look like my dad, but with more hair. She says, "He sold me on his dreams too and I married him, but now I'm raising you on my own while he has a free meal ticket at Club Fed."

The disillusionment and resentment follow me through the rest of high school as I labor through classes and high school drama. I end up cynical before I graduate.

With my dad in prison, my mom skeptical of my future, and no real friends other than Dr. Osgood, my pickup truck is the only part of my life that provides daily unquestioning loyal support. I still have that used truck, my version of a family legacy and a promise of freedom. It is sun-bleached, blotchy, and the floor is rusted out by road salt. When kids see that, they joke that I get my truck started by sticking my feet through holes in the floor and running like Fred Flintstone. These days we compare everything to a TV show.

In melt season when the roads are wet, I cover the holes in the floor to avoid getting splashed. My dad had told me how to get carpet samples from the store by pretending I was starting a home renovation. I lay them down over scrap plywood to survive the weather. In the summer I pull them out and watch the road underneath go by, like a repeating film strip of my short miserable life.

But still that truck is the only part of my life that works, even though the non-essential parts stopped working long ago and the windshield is cracked. Overall, it seems to fit my state of mind, beat-up, uninspired, limping, but not dead yet. With a worn-out muffler, it roars down the street as I accelerate. I call it my "angst rocket."

5

Ryder Scrapes Bottom

I feel desperate to break out somehow, so I apply to Illinois State to major in political science and get out of my mom's house. I tell her that I might take accounting so she will sign the papers on my student loans. I figure that my cynicism will work well in political science and my studies will distract me from my disillusioned personal state.

On my first day, I drive to the university in my beater pick-up truck. The unfamiliar setting opens my mind a little. I enroll at the registrar and walking out of the building I am suffused with hope and excitement about a new life. I walk around the campus on that first day marveling at the mysterious and powerful buildings and the advanced learning that must be going on inside. The upperclassmen and women seem full of purpose and potential. It feels like I can make a new start and I walk around, building a dream.

I sign up for a full load of classes including English, History, English History, and Political Science 101. I even wonder about maybe going pre-law. I commit to engage fully in my new life.

However, after a few months of hard work, I realize that there is no science involved in political science. That is a lie. Most of the politics the teachers talk about are just petty academic spats between professors. Meanwhile, national politics makes no sense at all, even worse, they kind of make anti-sense. Just lies about lies. I slump back towards disillusionment and cannot believe what passes for leadership and, more importantly, followership in our country. I decide to stop reading the news.

My other classes don't help much. After all, who cares about the English? It seems like all the major catastrophes in our world can be traced back to the British Isles. Without their penicillin and steam engines we would probably still be riding horses in a vibrant natural world facing a new glacial age instead of climate armageddon. Then they get all hoity toity while writing dramas about their damn kings and queens.

Finally, one day my poly-sci professor tells me in front of the class that I am under investigation for faking my assignments. Writing is the only outlet I have, so for once I speak up.

"Argh gack erk … WHAT? No!"

He says, "I will be making an example of you to our other students. Your papers are obviously professional while you never contribute anything in class. Until now I was not even sure you could talk."

I say, "That's not true," not yet thinking about how it would have helped me if I lied more often.

"Well, it is out of my hands now," he says with a vindictive smirk on his face. "You are on cautionary status. Maybe you should consider Ag school."

Then on my way out of the classroom that day, I see Agent Fred lurking in the hallway in his dark suit. He points his finger at me like a gun and pulls the trigger. I feel attacked. I look at him with a mixture of fear and truculence. I turn to walk the other way, but he is between me and the exit stairway. So, I lock down my emotions and start walking towards him.

As I am passing him by, looking down, he says to me, "So now you know what I can do to you. Think of me like I'm a natural disaster, powerful and inevitable. Now, how about giving up your dad's stash? Just get me the numbers and I will give you a cut."

I get pissed off.   Channeling one of my woke professors, I dig at him with, "You must have been one of the agents that sent the Chicago cops in to kill Black Panthers while they slept. How many other times did you start a gun battle so you could kill blacks while dressing it up as counter-intelligence? Did you just get an FBI salary for that? I guess that makes you both evil and a chump. Maybe you should run for office."

Fred's face turns red as he grimaces. "How could you know …? You don't…" Then he says, chastened, "You're right about being a chump, but back then I was an agent, now I am beyond that and I am free to use a wider range of my considerable skills."

In a more aggressive tone he says, "All it took for me to give you the shaft was inserting part of your text into a published paper and then sending the professor a link. That was easy and I am just getting warmed up. We had you on fraud with your dad even though the court let you off. Next time your clueless budding career goes all the way down."

I lash back at him sarcastically, "So I guess they fired you from the FBI. That must feel good."

Then, suddenly, I fake left and go right, dashing past him. He starts chasing me to the stairs, but I am faster this time. As the door to the stairs bangs open behind me, he howls, "Get me those numbers, or else."

I run down the stairs, angry. I transition to despair as I hustle out of the building. I feel a sharp pain in my midsection like I have been skewered by some kind of voodoo food poisoning. My entire life flashes by me as a series of crushed dreams followed by periods of cynical survival. Every time, I promise myself a new future and every time it is a lie.

I walk across campus simmering in depression and despair. Then my rebellious streak comes out again. I turn to go direct to the registrar to quit school. That damn Fred Arally can't take a career that I don't have or even want.

The next day I go around to personally inform all my professors, like they care. I follow my schedule, going up to each professor to tell them I am out. I bring my fart cushion along to punctuate my departures.

At the end of the day, I am hanging out in the school central plaza under the breezily waving trees stirred by a sweet wind off the lake, taking a last look at the campus. I look up at the stately buildings around me, feeling sad and wistful for the death of another dream.

Then three classmates come by. I know them well enough to say hi. They surround me, saying, "We heard, now let's celebrate."

I look at them and grumble, "You mean I should celebrate failure?"

Then thinking about defying my tormentors I say, "Well OK, as long as it involves drinking. Why not?"

We walk off campus to a college bar. The dark décor has picnic tables shiny from use and beer polish. The smell of stale beer is pungent along with a smell of old cigarette smoke that must be impregnated in the walls from back when. We get set up with beers and one of my classmates says, "You know, we envy your courage."

"Really," I say looking down, "What's so courageous about getting shafted and then quitting?"

"It is not the quitting part; it's going out into the real world. What are you going to do? The rest of us are happy to take classes, pick-up women, and write bullshit papers. Who cares if we can't repay the loans? All we have to do is ask intentionally stupid questions in class so the professors get to act smart."

That reminds me of my mom's suggestion about going out into the "real" world. But what is the real world? Is it as boring as the type-cast people fooling themselves all around me? Is it a criminal world where goons like my friendly ex-FBI agent extort people? Or is it scraping together a life around here in a place that I don't even like thinking about?

I dissent, "I am sorry to tell you this, but there is no real world, just different bubbles. Some are prettier than others but all are going to pop eventually, just like my late attendance at Illinois State. If you like a life full of PC bullshit, then go for it. Write those papers. Keep doing what you're doing. Meanwhile, let's drink."

Little did I know then that when I found my best life, it would be literally overflowing with bullshit.

6

Get Back on That Horse

Two weeks later I am laying on my bed in a bleary alcoholic semi-consciousness. I flinch when I hear a loud "bang, bang, bang." Is that the door? Deeply hung over, I gingerly rotate my legs over the edge of the bed. As my feet drag me upright, I notice that I am still wearing my jeans. When did I put them on, a week ago? And who have I been drinking with, anybody?

I rotate up to lean over my feet, nearly balanced. I am slowly unbending, but not sure why. Then I hear "bang, bang, bang" again. I shuffle from the bed to the door across the worn carpet, gingerly carrying my head to avoid the pain. The light seems unnaturally bright for early morning. I open the door a crack but leave the chain on.

I see cigarette-browned teeth in a grimace framed in wrinkles and a halo of thin, fly-away white hair. Oh god, the landlady. She's wearing a neon-bright, floral print, house coat and white pants like she just got back from the tropics. She hurts my eyes. She has a black cane strangled in her right hand as her main support.

One of her oversize side pockets carries a scrawny, growling, tan pocket dog. The dog has large beady eyes, long sparse hairs around black lips, and is gritting its teeth. Nasty.

"Rent," she says.

"Izzat your dog or a rabid badger," I stall.

Her pocket animal starts to growl, then barks, and yaps. His spittle sprays on my bare feet. Looking down, … ouch, my brain hurts. Then I think, no, that thing is too articulate to be a badger. I muse about whether she adopted an abnormally large and intelligent Norwegian Rat, thinking it was cute.

"Rent now," she elaborates.

"Wait 'til I wake up," I grumble.

"It's after 1 pm now," she retorts.

After a confused moment squinting aside at the bright daylight coming through the window in my apartment (oh look, it's midday), I dig into my jeans and pull out a balled-up mass of ones and fives. I shove this out through the crack of the door and grunt, "More later."

She takes the money and goes on, "You better get me the rest, or I am calling on my brother. He's gonna kick your ass."

I have bigger problems than her brother. He is older than she is and long retired from muscle work. I have seen him holed up in her apartment in a wheel chair with an oxygen tank. I wonder if he started out as a jock or a jerk, but he is too old for me to tell.

Meanwhile, I have to get out of here. Fred Arally and my landlady are making my future look homeless and dim. Also, I don't like the idea of sliding further into alcoholism since it seems like just another version of a high school doper.

I move to shut the door on her. Unfortunately, she shoves her cane into the crack of the door at the bottom and sticks her growly face up close. Man, she's quick. Apparently, this is not her first rodeo. But the chain is still on since I've been there too.

I give up and trundle back to bed. She rattles the door and yells at me through the crack about the rent. When she seems to run out of steam I grunt again from the bed, "More later."

This can't go on. As I lay in the bed, I despair over my life. How did it come to this? Isn't life supposed to be grand and free? Well, it is apparently not free. I am too poor to make the rent.

Then I agonize over failure. My dad always seemed to pull out of it with a new obsession, another idea with great potential. While my mom would be worried about getting new tires. Meanwhile my dad found that potential in prison and my mom was still changing out her old tires with retreads.

Two hours later I drag myself out of bed and sit down, depressed, at my computer to invent a resume. I might as well get after this; school isn't going to take me anywhere and I am not about to start helping my dad launder money just to end up where he is. I know I can bash this out since persistence is my only claim to success.

Meanwhile, I have to balance my cynicism with practicality. If everyone else can lie, I can do that too. I decide to apply for jobs where it is OK to just make stuff up instead of working. Ahhh yes, journalism. All I need is just enough fact to make it look good, like a poli-sci paper.

I spend a few moments looking out the window at the wispy clouds and dim late-winter sun. My anguish over abandonment and failed dreams has been building in me so long it has hardened in my heart. My thinking has been locked down by emotional hurt. No way will that attitude get me a job. I have to flip the script, pull it inside-out.

So, I shut down the hurt, and whip out a resume with a fantasy journalism degree and a juiced-up history. The ethical freedom of poverty helps me build a delusion of self-worth. It begins to be a little fun to describe my imagined credentials. Maybe I can still make a new start. Then I remember that I tried that before, so I know it doesn't work.

But at least I can get away from here, to somewhere that people think differently.

As you will see, it seems that I achieve that.

7

Ryder Goes West

I apply to work for starvation wages at local newspapers and advertising circulars across the country, really anything, anywhere else. I am persistent, sending out resumes all over. After a couple of weeks of nail-biting delay, lying to my mom, and deferring payments on my student loans, I get oddly excited and anxious about my only offer. I will be a roving reporter for the nearly unknown but aggressively literary Anderson Valley Advertiser (AVA) in Mendocino County, California. Their actual motto: "Fanning the Flames of Discontent." Perfect.

Aside from being somewhere else, their motto suggests a balance between enthusiasm and disappointment that looked like up to me. Kind of like how zero degrees looks when you have been at twenty below for a week on the tormented winter shores of lake Michigan. Based on the salary offer and my intention to take it, both the AVA and I are desperate and poor.

When I tell my mom that I have a job and need a bridge loan, she looks at me funny. "An actual job?" She looks a little skeptical but at least not dismissive. Her worry lines quiver and I think maybe she will miss me.

"No," she says, "I can't do it."

"Yes mom, an actual job. Well, at least they made an offer and I accepted…. but it is out in California so it may be a while before I see you. I'll call."

"You know," she says then, "my dream was to live somewhere on the west coast someday. But everyone told me that they were all fruits and nuts out there. So don't join some weird cult or nothing. Find a good steady girl."

Then after thinking a moment, she says, "OK, maybe I can do this, but it is the last money you get. You are cleaning me out."

Late the next week I enter my apartment building quietly, after dark. I have heard the ding that sounds when the door in the lobby opens to the downstairs parking garage. So, thinking ahead, I wedge the door open and head up to my room.

Later in the early morning silence, I creep down past the landlady's apartment. I can hear her brother's respirator through the thin door. I breathe quiet relief when I see that the garage door is still wedged. Any sound now and I will get busted. I walk out the door and down the stairs. I enter the cavernous parking area and the bright light exposes me, but the quiet then echoes my careful footsteps. I drive my trusty pickup to the door at the bottom of the stairs.

On my third trip down from my room, I stumble and drop a box of stuff in the lobby, spilling my stuff out on the floor.

I freeze and listen as the respirator reacts. Then the yapper starts growling low. I feel terror waiting for someone to wake up and halt my escape.

Then the respirator goes back into rhythm and the dog quiets down. OK, ... I reload the box quietly thinking I don't need the rest of my stuff. I pad quietly out the door, leaving the wedge in place.

I drive away surreptitiously to avoid paying the rent and dealing with the aged harridan and her vicious yapper. Even the muted thrum of my tires on the pavement makes me nervous. I keep my lights out as I coast down the road. I escape quietly, feeling guilty again. I promise myself to pay my back-rent later.

Heading out at sunrise through a Midwest haze, I pull off the freeway for fuel at a truck stop outside of Chicago. As always, when entering a gas station with an empty tank, I feel desperate at first then transition to faint hope as my tank fills up. Thinking back about my life and home, it all seems crazy. What happened to the beautiful and loving mom, wise and hardworking dad, two kids, and comical sidekick friend that life is supposed to be? I guess I wasn't cut out to be Beaver Cleaver.

The bland familiarity of the Two Partners Truck Stop, the fast food, fluorescent lights still lit in the sunrise, and extensive pavement feels deeply unnatural and yet completely normal. Even my truck seems to fit in while also rebelling against the lifeless freeway habitat. I load up with gas, a burner phone, and trail mix. Then I put my old phone on the back of a truck going somewhere else to distract my dear ex-agent Arally.

I batten down the hatches and stop thinking. I log into a fake account I got from my dad on my new phone and set up my route without any real knowledge of where I am going. I just gotta keep that little ball on the blue line. I continue to avoid thinking about the past and my upbringing as I take the shortest route across the plains toward my future.

8

The Ghost of Jefferson

Eventually, roaring freeways turn into long lonely western roads that are mostly paved and span wide open sage basins and dry dusty mountains. My truck rumbles along through sunsets and sunrises and I camp out on back roads, sleeping in my pickup bed in all of my clothing. Finally, I find myself after a long drive looking into the blazing afternoon sun as I roll through partly burned pines and firs into the town of Yreka, California.

I stop for a rest and a bite at the Yreka Bakery. The store is filled with the intoxicating aroma of bread and sugar. The Yreka Bakery, "it's a palindrome!" one of my ex-professors would have squeaked. Approximating that spirit, I order Ye Talle Latte and peer at the bulletin board on a wall at the end of a long glass bakery case across an ancient dusty white tile floor.

I think, how quaint, a bulletin board. Walking over to the board, I see a used truck for sale, junk hauling service, last month's county fair, and a faded notice for a meeting every Thursday of the Patriotic Revolution Committee at the Bad Cowboy Bar. A little startled, I look at the notice again and then at the server behind the glass case, "What's this about a revolution?"

She is older than my mom, with grey lanky hair and an old lady body, not fat, but dumpy and re-shaped by age. She is wearing an old-fashioned waitress dress in pink and white stripes with her name on an embroidered patch, Yvonne. She looks up at me like I wasn't from around there.

"Ahh," she says, "You are not yet acquainted with the "raison de etre" of our community, our past history of greatness, and our excuse for drinking. We are committed believers in the Patriotic Revolution of the State of Jefferson." She leans down to pick up a pamphlet from a pile on the counter. "Here, take this pamphlet from the town council." Surprised that she can quote French, I sit down in a booth to read it.

The pamphlet says, "The Patriotic Revolution of the State of Jefferson flowered in the fervent hearts of the citizens of northern California and southern Oregon in late 1941. The movement broke out in direct action among residents, blocking roads and demanding donations and statehood in protest of the neglect by state governments for this forgotten region. They just wanted to be free."

Right, me too. Then I wonder idly how they could be free if they were charging tolls.

It continues, "Stanton Delaplane, then a cub reporter, reported on the secessionist movement in the pages of the San Francisco Chronicle. He is rumored to have written the revolutionary manifesto himself while visiting Yreka. Delaplane's work inspired NBC News to travel north from Hollywood to embellish the revolution on film. They recorded a festive parade and a few staged events with clean, well-dressed revolutionary cowboys setting up professionally-printed signs from horseback. Delaplane's missives, for which he received the Pulitzer Prize, were printed at the bottom of the front page of the Chronicle below the banner headlines of the time screaming about Hirohito, Mussolini, and Roosevelt in November and early December of 1941.

"After December 7, the Patriotic Revolution was postponed for the war in the Pacific, although, according to the original manifesto: patriotic Jeffersonians intend to secede each Thursday until further notice." Ahh, I think, The meeting at the bar.

All this sounds to me like a long-lost political movement full of misbegotten righteous anger dressed up as ideals. I heard about plenty of that from my professors. No doubt it fizzled and came to nothing out here like everywhere else. Now it's just another excuse for drinking. I could relate to that.

I ask Yvonne, "So is this a meeting for the local historical society?"

Yvonne responds, "Oh no. We are all about current events. Five counties in northern California have already submitted declarations of separation from the state and more will follow. We still need to build up our fortitude some, so we meet at the bar."

Then I think, today is Thursday, so why not?

I check into an old highway motel to get a shower, for once.

Early that evening I head over to the Bad Cowboy, which is just another low, flat-roof bar beside the road with a faded sign showing a cowboy on a bucking horse. It might have lit up in colorful neon once, but now the only lights on the sign that I see are the reflections of headlights passing on the road. It reminds me of my childhood dreams, once in color, but now dim and broken. There are a few pickups parked outside so my truck has company. As I approach the entry, I notice the dusty window on the door is cracked and secured by plastic tape.

Walking into the bar, I scan the crowd. Nobody seems to notice my arrival… maybe because their heads are down, which is probably a good thing. The music is sad country, some guy singing about his dog in the rain. I find myself at the end of the bar and get a beer to have something to do while eavesdropping on the conversation.

Nobody says much. My neighbor isn't talking much either. He is young but old and wearing a cowboy shirt worn under the elbows. He has a grizzly beard, too long to be movie-sexy but too thin to be a real beard.

He looks at me and asks, "Where you from?"

I say, "No place good. I am on the run from my past and unsure of the future. I stopped in here to find out what this place has going on." Then I ask, "Where are the *good* cowboys?"

My neighbor mumbles, "They don't come in here. It's all big spreads now. They keep to themselves mostly. And there ain't no cowboys in here at all, we drive trucks."

"What happened to the State of Jefferson?"

"This is it," he says.

"Are you all getting ready for the uprising?" I ask, provocatively.

He says, "We all are still up at this point, though usually some of us will be laying down on the sidewalk later. Meanwhile, nobody is going to be rising, we're stuck down here with you, getting drunk 'cause it reminds us of the fun we had as kids."

"So, when is the revolution?"

"Oh, the politicians will talk that up before the next election. Don't mean nothing. They have nothing else to talk about."

That seemed to sum it up pretty well, entirely consistent with my life. As almost-a-truck-driver, I identify with his frustrated attitude. I shuffle out of the bar concluding that the State of Jefferson is a state of inebriation leading to a sidewalk black-out and is reduced to political talking points not much different from politics elsewhere, just lies and hype.

I return to my motel to sleep in thin sheets. My room looks worn, like any old motel, but still luxurious after days of sleeping rough. It feels anonymous and tentative like time is suspended and so for a moment, I am outside my depressing life.

In the moments before sleep, I contemplate my private disparagement of the Patriotic Revolution of the State of Jefferson, but I neglect to consider the power of the future. Although the future is always a dream, it is partly based on fact, like much of the news today.

9

Far-Out West

After driving west across the rest of northern California the next day, I approach the town of Arcata. I can smell the ocean through the open window, as well as in the breeze that comes through the floor of my truck. I have never been to the ocean. So, when I see a sign for Dune Beach, I take the turnoff.

I go down a long single lane gravel road through a field of coastal grass taller than my truck with dense low trees hanging above. It is dark and green. My truck tires growl at the gravel as I crawl through the narrow tunnel. After about ten minutes, I see lighted openness ahead. I drive into a small parking lot. Towering white dunes sparkle ahead in full sunlight and bleach my eyes.

I step out of my truck squinting, stretching out the ache from the long drive. The parking lot has a thin dusting of sand from the dunes that crunches under my feet. The only other vehicle is a painted-up van with a pile of stuff on a roof rack and jerry cans hanging on the back doors. I hear voices and the faint tinkling of wind chimes and walk over to the van. A man and woman are lounging in folding beach chairs on the dune side of the van under a fringed awning. A pot is steaming on a cook stove on the small table between them.

"Where's the beach?" I ask.

Looking at them now, they are both thin and dressed entirely in dingy white rough cotton with matching long scraggly blondish hair. The woman has a sneaky kind of grin like she has a secret life. She speaks first, "You have reached the end of the civilized world, my friend. All paths from here must be made your own. Follow the sound of the surf through the shifting sands of your future to learn who you can become."

I immediately think of my mom's warning. This woman sounds either deeply indoctrinated in new age philosophy or just high.

The man then says, "You have not yet arrived and must persist on your journey. Do not tarry lest you find yourself stillborn on the way to creation."

These people do not fit into the panoply of my high school cliques. I think maybe they are Jesus Freaks. I am uncertain what this means or what to do.

The man then enigmatically says, "We bother with neither drugs nor religious dogmas. We are here to learn. They would just get in the way." Then he points to the dunes.

I think, how did he know what I was thinking about them? Then I turn to the dunes confused. I feel the deep reverberation of surf and start walking toward the thunder and light.

As I reach the sand, my shoes begin to sink as I trudge to the slope of the dunes. I start climbing toward a low point. I look up at the horizon above me, up the bright sand to a crest outlined in blue. As the slope steepens, I begin to slide and sink deep so my shoes are filling with sun-warmed sand. I sit down to take off my shoes. Looking back to the east, it appears that the van has already left the parking lot. That was quick.

I continue up the slope, gripping the sand between my toes and breathing heavily with the effort of sinking while climbing. My mind shuts down from the effort as I slowly struggle up. Finally reaching the top, breathing hard, my blood rushing, I am not sure how long it took to climb.

But then I look down at the Pacific. The blue water is white-capped and mists of spray are blowing off the top of the waves toward the beach. The thunder of the massive breakers speaks to my chest while the hiss of the foam as it races up the sand makes a white noise that finally eclipses the sounds of my tires still lingering in my ears. I am alone.

Carefree for once, I race down the dune, each long stride carries me sliding with the flow of sand around me. Exuberant, I race to the firm wet sand at the shore, strip off my clothes, and rush laughing into the water.

After a moment of delirious celebration, I get bowled over and thrashed by a big breaker. Jesus Fucking Christ, it's cold!

The wave carries me in some. I resurface, salt water sluicing off, while my vision returns. I stand up on the sand, blow the water from my lips, take a few breaths, and walk back to the beach through the flowing water, lifting my feet above the water, each in turn, shivering. I reach firm sand, turn, and sit in the sun to watch the waves.

After a moment of reflection, I hear, "Congratulations, you made it."

I turn and the blonde couple are standing right behind me. I see their van up the beach.

I ask, "So there's a road?"

The woman responds, "Yes, but it was not on your path."

"Well, you might have told me."

She says, "But it matters how you arrive. Finding your own path helps you create who you become."

Walt adds, "It is about personal struggle on your way to self-realization… We can give you a ride back when you are ready."

They walk off down the beach and I turn back to the waves and think about how I got here. The sun is going down and lights the streaking clouds. The display of deep natural color is almost a revelation. This is a long way from the Two Partners Truck Stop.

As the sunset darkens, I stand to look at the ocean one more time and turn inland. The misty breeze is chilling so I put my clothes back on.

They are waiting for me sitting cross-legged next to the van. They have a small driftwood fire going, so I sit down and look across the flames. They are dishing up some stew and offer me a wooden bowl.

The woman looks at me and says, "I'm Coco and this is Walt. What did you learn today?"

"Well, this is the first time I have seen the ocean and a sunset like that."

Walt then asks, "Yes, but beyond that?"

I think for a minute and say, "I saw the curve of the planet."

"Yes again," Walt agrees quietly. Then he says louder, "Now that you see the world, you have to suspend disbelief to know it."

I think, what does that mean? Is this an epic moment? I shouldn't listen to his spacy new wave aphorisms. But then, are they any crazier than where I come from?

Coco suggests I take a shower from a hose on the back of their van. I strip down again and feel the life-giving energy of fresh water on my skin. The ocean salt flows into the sand at my feet. There is no towel, so I shake off the water like a bear rising from the river.

Reborn and redressed I come back out to the fire and sit down cross-legged.

After a conversation about our life stories, we all sleep in sand warmed from the day and the fire. Coco offers me a worn but clean-looking wool blanket. I pull it over me and sleep, untroubled.

In the morning, they open the back of the van and climb into the front seats. I lay on the mattress in the back and look at the colorful hanging fabrics and boxes. Their van smells like incense and chicken soup.

The man looks back at me and says simply, "Our worldly goods." He turns back to drive through the sand.

They drop me off in the parking lot next to my pick-up. As I get out of the van, I feel a swell of gratitude and tell them, "Thank you, my name is Ryder, thanks for the ride and ... everything."

As I watch them go, I am not sure what just happened. One thing is clear, I am not in Chicago anymore.

I leave the beach and drive south toward Mendocino. As I pass through the early spring-time redwoods, the sunlight filters through the majestic and patient trees to the deep green carpet below. I think back to my odd experience at the ocean.

Although I am still the depressed cynic from Chicago out to scratch up a living in hiding by writing made-up stories, I have another somewhat detached sense that maybe I am not the same cynic. Remembering the woman at the beach I think, what did she mean: "Who I can become"? I reject that thought immediately. I know better than to buy into that new age pseudo-psycho bullshit.

Meanwhile what was going on with Coco and Walt? They must be nuts.

10

The Anderson Valley Advertiser

As I roll into Anderson Valley in my still surviving beater truck, I notice the change to rolling hills, grasses, vineyards, and oak woodland. I arrive in Boonville, a town whose small wood buildings seem to suspend time. The buildings are covered in wood siding and there is a plank sidewalk under a veranda roof along the road.

The address I'm looking for is on the one street that comes off the main road. The taller wood building standing there has not been painted lately and old lettering in faded paint on the outside suggest that it has been a warehouse and feed store in previous lives. I hear a repetitive rumbling and knocking coming from inside.

I stand on the street a moment, on the brink of the future.

The moment passes and I find a door between windows that are painted white on the inside. Upon knocking, again, the door opens to a tall, powerful man with a robust red beard and a bow tie. The clanking behind him is loud. He is strangely wearing dark sunglasses indoors with a plaid country shirt, pressed jeans, and cowboy boots. "You must be our new reporter," he says, "Come on in."

"And you must be Bruce Anderson, editor. Did I get that right?"

"Yes, come in, come in."

Inside the building the noise is ferocious, so we have to shout. An old-fashioned press is slamming away, the high windows are dusty on the inside and some have cobwebs. Several people are working at desks or caring for equipment all spread out in a single warehouse space. All in all, it is impressive, although I am not sure which century I am in.

He leads me to an inner office, which is blissfully quieter. The man is a talker, which relieves me from remembering the lies I put in my resume. He describes their focus and printing process while waving his arms. I begin to feel that he is either the real deal, thoroughly deluded, or both.

He says, "I am a socialist and an anarchist, but I welcome other ideas when they are clearly expressed. I am looking forward to changing your mind."

I tell him, "Socialism and anarchy are actually mutually exclusive, so it seems you are also open-minded and not prone to the agony of cognitive dissonance."

I cringe at my own words, where did that come from? I am sure to get thrown out. Perhaps part of a political science education is worse than none.

But he responds, "Whooopee! You noticed! We are going to get along fine."

"So, I can start?" I ask, not believing it.

"Yes, now, would be good. Go next door to the café and pick up some juicy gossip, then run down the facts." Then he says, "Just do your journalism gig, tell mostly the truth, and make it interesting. Find some stuff out and fan the flames."

Finally, some enthusiasm. I am not sure that it matters what it is about.

I walk out of the office a little stunned by the noise, conversation, and my new position. I turn and walk into the Boonville Café next door. I am hungry from the drive. Maybe I can eavesdrop while eating pie.

The café is old, the wood tables are old on a plank floor, and the menus look old, but the waitress is young, maybe a couple years older than I am. She attracts the eye with mid-length, straight, light brown hair, casual clothes, tights, and a smile that has the promise of much better than I am used to. She motions with her head to an open table. Actually, all of the tables are open other than one in the back corner where two men in overalls are drinking coffee and grumbling.

I sit down and look at the menu. No pie.

The waitress bops over with some kind of inner rhythm and says, "My name is Anita. Lunch?"

"What do you have?"

"Any kind of sandwich that we can make with the stuff we got."

"OK, that narrows it down. I'll have one of those."

She says then, "Do you want something on the side, like soggy fries or maybe a nice fat pickle?"

"Just the sandwich."

"Well, think it over, I love me a fat pickle."

She leaves to make my sandwich and I watch her walk away. Oh my, that helps my attitude tremendously. After that I tune into the conversation in the back.

The two men are leaning back, drinking coffee. They are wearing ranch clothes and look like they have been there a long time. One is tall and the other short. Did the dust settle on their clothes while they were sitting at the table? Their broad brimmed hats sit on the other two chairs, also dusty.

The tall man says to the other, "*Russell's broadies are tongue-cupping and eatin' lizards. Een boss broadie ain't burlapping nemer. Russell been killing snake to bring them 'long.*"

What? Did I hear that right? Does he have a speech impediment or do I have a hearing glitch? I ask, "What's going on?"

The short man responds, "Oh, he's *harping Boontling*, a local dialect. You don't get it 'cause you're not from here."

"That's right, I am just in town and working for Mr. Anderson at the Anderson Valley Advertiser. My name is Ryder."

"In that case, since you work for Bruce," the short man says with a tolerant grin, "He's just saying there are some sick cattle up in Willits."

Although I am completely ignorant about cattle beyond cowboy movies and childhood dreams, I am nevertheless drawn to the image of a noble rancher with cow trouble. This is real stuff, nothing like politics, and although cows seem boring maybe this passes for news around here.

My sandwich comes back as a monster, with both green and red lettuce sticking out like an unruly hairdo capped under gnarly bread with a similarly sized pickle on the side.

"You weren't kidding about the pickle," I say to the waitress. "Where'd you get this thing."

"Oh, I raise and pickle 'em myself. You'll love it."

"Well, thanks."

She walks off and I turn my attention again to the back table and butt into their conversation again, "Where in Willits?"

"Ok you best be talking to Russell Brand; we don't know nothing much about it. He runs cattle up there, southeast of Willits."

I leisurely finish my sandwich and wait for the waitress to show up again.

I say, "I loved that sandwich."

She has hazel eyes. "Well then, come again," she says.

I notice that I am looking forward to paying the bill. This doesn't seem like me.

11

Plenty of Bullshit

I rumble in my truck up to Willits. Asking around, I find the road to a ranch house southeast of town at the base of the hills. I drive up a long gravel driveway into a dirt yard in front of the house and get out of my truck. Thinking about the ranch etiquette that I learned from the movies, I stand out in the yard and holler, "Hello, Mr. Brand?"

The house is dark weathered pine with a covered front porch and a few outbuildings. An old stick fence encloses the yard and the barn. I can hear chickens and a dog. Sunlight slants down across the house through big Valley Oaks.

After a long moment, a crusty looking man in dungarees and a plaid shirt steps out of the barn. He is lean and a bit bow-legged but clean-shaven. His eyes are deep blue. "Who's asking?" he says.

"I'm Ryder Jeffers from the Anderson Valley Advertiser. I'm here to ask you about cattle."

"Bruce sent you, ehh? Well, I know about cattle. Come on up on the porch. But don't bother asking me about the other Russell Brand. He don't live here."

I notice him step off his boots beside the stairs. So, I kick off my shoes and climb to the porch in my holey, college-student socks.

We have a long and wandering conversation about cow disease. I ask a lot of questions and he answers a few words at a time or rambles on at length.

After a while, his wife comes out and smiles like she knows Russell is important and is glad to see somebody on her side. She has tied-up hair and jeans. She offers coffee. As Ms. Brand goes back into the house, she gives me a wink. I begin to think I should have been born here.

I ask Russell, feeling oddly hopeful, "So do you ever work from horseback?"

"I got to," he says. "The hills are steep and if I had roads, they would wash out.… Why, do you like horses?"

"Oh, I used to ride some. Can I meet them?"

We walk out to the barn and I greet his horses. They seem friendly and the barn is well-kept. Hay bales are stacked in the back and the stalls look clean. Light comes through gaps between the siding boards so everything is striped with sunlight, including the hay dust floating in the air. It feels warm and smells like hay and animals.

I notice that one of the horses is a palomino. "Where did you get her?" I ask.

"We've got a breeder south of Willits. He provides me with working horses, the ones that don't make the grade for racing or shows. They all have good blood though. This one's named Aragorn after the wanderer king in the Hobbit."

He gives me a carrot which I turn and give to the horse. As Aragorn nibbles at my hand, Russell says, "My horse is Rama, the Hindu god."

He asks If I ride. Then he points to a saddle and bridle. "Let's mount up and I can show you how bad it has gotten with the herd."

Russell sure gets me started. After riding with him and meeting his herd, I follow up with disease experts to get background on his sick cows. Later I file my first report for the newspaper.

Fanning the Flames of Discontent

Cattle Diarrhea in Willits

By Ryder Jeffers, reporter for the AVA

An illness has been affecting range cattle in Little Lake Valley near Willits. Russell Brand, a local rancher, hails from an old Mendocino ranching family and looks the part, wearing boots and a big hat. His boots are stained dark and he has a faint odor of cow and horse.

He commented that his cattle have been looking thin and there is a lot of very liquid stool around. He said, "Cow patties can always be a little runny, but now they are forming streams that gather up and rush down the hill. You got to keep an eye peeled around the herd or the flow can slip you off your feet. I called the state but they never get back to me. Then I found an expert. I have to do something because I can't sell the meat if it ain't on the cow. Plus it is getting as slippery as … well you know."

Your intrepid reporter chased down his expert. Cal Fartze was contacted by phone at his home in Sacramento. Mr Fartze is the former director of pest control for the State Dept. of Conservation. Mr. Fartze started out as a contract nozzle head, spraying pests for the state, and rose up like a poisonous mist through the ranks to director, emeritus. Now he consults. "I have a degree in entomology," he said, "so I know more than you do about this shit."

He remembered a similar infestation of cow diarrhea in Arizona some years ago. "It was serious at the time. They quarantined the range and were treating them with initial success before a fire swept through the area and eradicated the disease. Anyway when Mr. Brand called me, I dredged through my files and put him in contact with the vet from Arizona."

Dr. Diana Rhia is a bovine intestinal veterinarian and entrepreneur. She was trained at the College for Homeopathic Animal Alternatives. She arrived in Willits to deal with the disease along with her brother, Conner, and her partner, Annie Malls.

Miss Malls said they plan to open a store in a vacant building in the downtown. "Look for us soon in Willits," she said. "We are opening a storefront to provide veterinary services and equipment. We plan to call it Diana Rhia's Agricultural Emporium."

When asked about treating the disease, Dr. Rhia said that intestinal disease is rare in cattle. "So, there aren't many experts and we are always running around. When it starts to flow, we gotta go."

She said that treatment for intestinal disease is straightforward. "To put it in simple terms, we treat them from one end and then plug up the other to keep it from spreading.

"The virus thrives in stomach acid so we use massive doses of antacid to raise stomach pH. Getting the antacids in deep enough to treat all four stomachs is a serious challenge. My brother, Conner, adapted beer bong technology to get it done. His device flushes the antacids in deep. It turns out he did learn something useful in college."

Conner added, "We are now testing an advanced version that I call the Cow Bong 500 – Turbo®. I figured we could better maintain flow integrity using vortex technology so I added a turbulator on the bong flow line. A turbulator is a simple spiral vane inside the pipe that gets the fluid spinning. The vortex integrity helps send the medicine past the first chamber and through to the third. The beauty is that these turbulators are cheap and off the shelf. Then I added a Venturi on the line to suck in the antacid. It uses the Bernoulli principle to get better mixing.

"You still gotta start by feeding the cow long hay and then grain to delay eructation of their cud while being treated. You don't want them to spit it out."

Diana elaborated, "To plug up the other end, I use my proprietary Super-Swell® anal suppository. My patent deals with the pattern of the threads on the one-size-fits-all wedge-shaped plug. The plug is based on clay and pectin like Kaopectate, but I added a couple of secret ingredients to increase swell volume.

"It is a little tricky to get my suppository in but the threads help avoid blow-back. I use slow, twisting, right hand wrist action and goggles. I am currently experimenting with a pull-down face mask like welders use, but with a windshield wiper.

"I like to play music so my patients are more receptive. They like Motown, especially Barry White. It helps them get in the mood."

Following up on the controversy in Arizona, I asked what happened. Dr. Rhia said, "We were having good success until the fire. Some of the cattle were even gaining weight.

"But when you plug up a cow, they still generate a lot of methane. Normally they just burp it out. In the excitement of the fire, the cows must have seized up and bloated with gas. You do not want to think about what happens when a gas-bloated cow like that gets near a flame.

"Anyway, fire fighters reported a long series of explosions that must have been my cows spreading the blaze. I am still traumatized by the whole affair. It's embarrassing when a herd of your patients goes out like that."

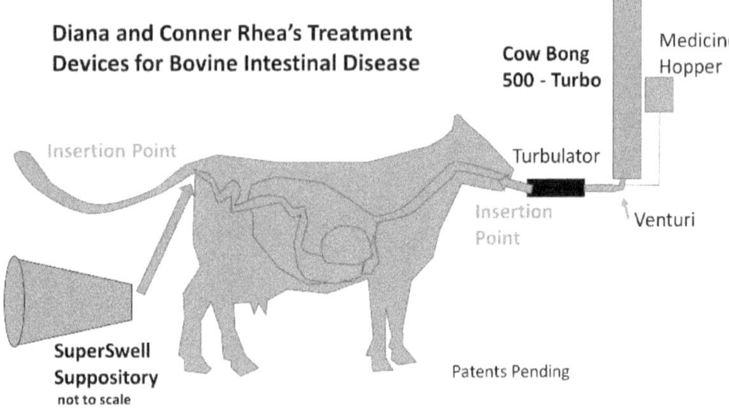

When I show my report to Mr. Anderson, he says, "Talk about fanning the flames! You are on fire, boy. Where did you dig this up?"

"I ran into some ranchers next door," I reply.

"Well, I like it. Your style reminds me of Dave Barry from the Miami Herald."

I love the compliment, my first in a while. I say, "Maybe Mendocino will become the Miami of California."

"Don't say that," he says, "We are not even close. Florida is where free speech goes to die and people actually bury their heads in the sand. We trend the other way."

Then he asks, "So did you meet that nice Miss Margarita next door?"

"You noticed," I quote him.

I think then of Anita. She is like an intoxicating dream of sweet chicken stew cooking in the kitchen where the flavors drift out in steamy waves. I am caught in the next room like a cartoon dog and am transported through the air following the smell. When I float into the kitchen, my eyes bug right out of my head on springs and back in when I see her.

Somehow my cynicism is momentarily gone and my self-perceived inadequacies don't matter. Yikes, what is brewing in my head? I do not know and I am powerless to resist.

"Well," Bruce interrupts my revery, "Your report looks great. I may have to make a few adjustments but we can run it tomorrow. It will be your first by-line with the AVA."

"Is it too long?" I ask. "I don't want to blither-on too much. Also, the veterinary methods they talked about sound odd. But what do I know? They make sense."

"Definitely not too long," Mr. Anderson avers. "We need copy that keeps people reading through the ad sections, that is to say, all of our sections. Long and odd are fine if it holds interest. Also, that means I don't have to write up some bullshit that everybody already knows about. We like fresh shit up here."

12

Accidents Happen

"Next assignment," Mr. Anderson says. "We can always get something from the sheriff. His name's Giles, Giles Teeman, but goes by Gil. You can find him at the Sheriff's Office in Ukiah. I'll call his secretary but you just go over tomorrow morning. He is pretty friendly in person."

I am beginning to appreciate that my beater truck is still alive, this work takes a lot of driving around.

I bed down at the Boonville Hotel, in the same building as the café. It's rustic but reasonable. The building is entirely made of redwood, the floor is made of huge planks from old growth. It is a little dingy and scuffed but the windows have bright curtains.

Through the window, I hear angry hollering from the bar next door. A little grumpy, I stomp down and ask about it at the hotel desk. The clerk says, "They call that bar the *Bucket of Blood* in *Boontling* 'cause of all the fighting. If you wait a bit they'll take the action out to the street to avoid messing the furniture." I return upstairs and it quiets down after the boys get what they want.

The next morning, I shuffle around my room getting ready, then trundle down the ancient wood stairs.

I can't help myself and stop at the café.

"Miss Anita Margarita, I am pleased to meet you."

"So, you have been doing your homework," she replies. "I don't remember giving my full name."

"Oh right, Bruce mentioned it. However, I have no home as yet. I am just into town and working for The Advertiser. You are the best part of this town so far."

"So far? You going somewhere?"

"Yes, well, If I knew where I was going, maybe I could ask you along."

"Maybe? You should work on your commitment skills."

"I will do that, but first I am headed to Ukiah to see the sheriff."

"Well then, call me if they let you out."

I drive to Ukiah from Boonville on the cutoff through rolling oak forest and grasslands. The road gets steep as I drop from the ridge into Ukiah Valley. The spring grasses are lush and the poppies are coming out. The quiet between towns sets me up to meet the sheriff.

The Sheriff's Office is also the jail and in the same building as road maintenance. The outside is that classic beige stucco that is supposed to look like colonial Mexico, but on a low flat-roof building it looks more like a cell block. There are a few parking places in front like they don't get many visitors. But then who goes to see the sheriff voluntarily?

When I walk into the building, a sign on an open door to the left says "Sheriff." Great. I get a look and a nod from his secretary and walk in.

"Hello," says a booming voice. Then he stands up, at least 6' 5", walks around his desk and offers a hand. I reach out to a muscular man with a big black and grey mustache erupting from his lip like a bank of untamed Jimson weed. He is dressed in a movie version of Texas Ranger. The room has reports stacked around but still smells like leather.

"I'm Gil Teeman," he says, "and before you ask, not!"

"Not? Not what?"

"Do I really have to tell you? Not guilty, man!" he laughs out loud. "Get it?" He says, "I took hell for that name in high school." Then he says to himself, "But why do I still laugh about it?"

"Limited intellect?" I mutter quietly.

"What good is intellect if you can't laugh?" He smiles.

Which may be the smartest thing I have heard since high school. It makes me chuckle about my snarky attitude.

"I got a call from Bruce 'bout you. He gets me all kinds of free advertising in that rag of his. He fans the flames and I put out the fires."

"Well then, what kind of police action can I report today?"

"Well, we had a truck crash into the Van Arsdale Reservoir last night. Who knows what freight they were carrying and that out there is the road to nowhere. So, you could go out and relieve some of the mystery."

"So, you want me to be a detective?" I ask.

"Did you say you're defective? Then yes, you'll do fine."

So, I am on the road again, chasing another story. It takes all day. I interview a range of different characters, not all of them are cooperative. Later I file the following report with Mr. Anderson.

Fanning the Flames of Discontent

Truck Sinks at Van Arsdale

By Ryder Jeffers, reporter for the AVA

Last Friday night a large panel truck crashed through a fence and into the Van Arsdale Reservoir, where the Eel River feeds the diversion of waters to the Russian River.

The sheriff's deputy at the scene, Buzz Mackey, described the aftermath. "I got there just after the accident. The truck flipped into the water and was missing one front wheel. There were skid marks on the road and the fence was laid down. I found the driver bruised and dazed on the side of the road. He was lucky he didn't go into the water and get sucked down the intake for the diversion tunnel to the Potter Valley power plant."

When asked what was in the truck the deputy said, "Not sure, but whatever was in that truck spilled out the back cause those doors were completely sprung."

The driver was taken to the hospital and was stunned but in stable condition. When this AVA reporter attempted to enter his room, I was stopped by his nurse. "We had to sedate him 'cause he keeps chasing the nurses," she said. "This guy is both deprived and depraved. Anyway, you can't go in, he's senseless now." She was interrupted by a roar from the room behind her. "Damn you," she said over her shoulder. "Well, I guess he's awake. But don't get too close, he doesn't seem to care about gender."

In the room the injured man had a bandage on his right hand and an IV in his arm. His wrinkled face was pale yellow and his hair was white and puffed up above his head from laying on the pillow. He looked like a slice of dried-up lemon meringue pie.

He refused to give his name. "Puddingtame," he said, "ask me again and I'll tell you the same." When I suggested that he might be briefly famous if I put his name in the paper, he relented and said "You can call me Whip."

I asked where he got that name. He told me his story, "Back in the sixties I used to scrape-by selling organic smoothies from a pushcart on the streets in San Francisco. So, one day a big white Lincoln Continental stops, you know, the kind with the back doors that open from the front, and a man steps out that I recognize as Bill Graham, the famous rock impresario from the Filmore Auditorium. I serve him my signature smoothie and jokingly ask if he would let me drive his car. He said, 'Well… I am looking for a driver.'

"Within a few weeks I was loading amps and guitars and driving a van full of musicians around to gigs in the Bay Area. It was a crazy life trying to drive around while band members were constantly feeding me LSD and Gatorade.

"At one point a drummer asks me how I got the job and I tell him 'Banana Whip', talking about my smoothie. The band loved that so much it became my name for long enough that I forgot my others. Anyway, I got a commercial truck driving license for that job and I've been driving trucks ever since."

When asked about the crash Whip said, "I was driving my truck. It's been a little funky lately. Ever since I parked it in the field by my house it smells like rat piss when I turn on the vents. They must be nesting in there.

"Anyway, I took it down to Arizona and was driving back with a load. I was overweight so I had to stay off the main roads. They were in a big rush to get this load to Willits so I had been on the road since dawn. Then I overheated.

Under the hood I saw that those rats had eaten through the radiator hose. That set me back a few hours in Calpela. I guess I should'a known them rats would get hungry after they got into my brownies.

"Leaving Calpela, I got lost turning off Highway 20. I wandered the back roads for a while, then I was driving past a narrow lake. Just then smoke started coming out from under the hood and I thought the damn rats must be eating the electricity.

"One was sticking his head out from under the hood, 'cause of the smoke. So, I leaned over to grab my gun outa the glove box. Reaching in, one of those damn rats bit my hand. So, I leaned back and let off a couple of rounds into the glove. Then I saw the other one stick his head out again from under the hood and I took it off with a couple more rounds. Pretty good shootin' I'd say.

"I was happy about that until I started choking from the smoke pouring through my shot-out windshield. I noticed that this was probably an unsafe situation. So, I grabbed my beer and bailed out the door. I watched my truck hit a rock and balance on two wheels for a sec. then slowly tumble into the lake. Lucky I still had a few sips left."

When asked what was in the truck he said, "Not sure, they were medical supplies for Dr. Rhia in Willits."

Contacted by phone, Dr. Rhia confirmed that her shipment was missing. "My entire load of cow suppositories," Ms. Rhia moaned. "I went up to try and salvage some but they were sucked down the intake."

When asked about the effect of the suppositories on water quality she said, "They are all natural ingredients, mostly clay and pectin. In any case the Eel will be fine because they went down the tunnel.

"Wait a minute, they must have swelled up in the flow. Oh no, there was probably enough in that truck load to plug the diversion tunnel."

As soon as I write this up, I send a copy to the sheriff figuring that he will appreciate the feedback.

He calls me immediately. "Whip was more eloquent with you compared to us. But there is no point in our tracking him down now. This may be California, but there is no statute against pest control from a moving vehicle."

My editor reads my report and then tells me that the big news here isn't the crash. "If the Eel diversion gets blocked, it will stir up a foofaraw. No, not just a foofaraw, it's going to be a full-on hulabaloo, a wild, mad hulabaloo. And we are gonna be there, stoking the fire.

"We have a committed group of Earth First revolutionaries around here, along with a fervent State of Jefferson cabal. Most were born out in the woods and their parents were either back-to-the-earth hippies or workers at the old lumber mill before it shut down. Used to be after high school guys would either join the army or work at the mill. Now that the mill is gone, all of them grow pot. None will be too friendly to repairing that unnatural diversion. They need the water for their grows.

"Two years ago, Caltrans was building a highway bypass around Willits that was delayed a year by Firsters living up in the trees in ghillie suits, those clothes that look like bushes that hunters wear. The sheriff refused to pull them down out of the trees, said it's protected free speech. That was just a kerfluffle in comparison to the hurly-burly that's gonna go down now."

Then Mr. Anderson says, his voice starting to rise, "Now that the water diversion is shut off, it should stay that way, dangnabit." He starts getting even more excited about it and as he talks, his face reddens like his hair. He stands and his voice grows, "This is our chance; this is our chance." Then he strides around the warehouse thundering to the staff, "Fan the Flames, dammit, Fan the Flames."

I am still new here, so I am a little surprised by the depth of feeling and the apparent radical attitudes of a rural community, even the sheriff. Revolution? I thought that was history.

13

The Movement

The next day my editor writes a long incitement to secession in his "Free Speech" column. "Why do we need those fools in Washington D.C. that control dam operation," he writes. "Sacramento is bad enough, but we can't afford roads and schools without them. What does DC do except pose for photos and suck up our taxes to give to their buddies to build bombs?"

I take his column next door to show Anita.

"How do you think the readers will respond to this?" I ask her.

"My guess, they are all-in."

"Really, all of them?"

"No, only about half, but that should be plenty. Get ready to rock."

"By the way," she says, "I have been reading your articles in the paper."

"Thanks,… I guess. What do you think?"

"I'm not sure yet, but at least they are more entertaining than the ads."

By next week when I make my daily visit to see Anita, the place is full and buzzing. I notice an eclectic fashion pattern, country jeans, tie dye shirts, boots, shorts, sandals, and bare feet, all manner of head gear from cowboy hats to berets and headbands, and hair from buzzcuts to dreads. I think, if fashion marks a revolution, then this one is bringing in all types. It looks like the movement style is going to be cowboy revolutionary, a combination of John Wayne and Che Guevara.

Talking with some of the people at the cafe suggests there are plenty of both right- and left-wing attitudes but no rancor. In fact, while the discussion is boisterous and loud, it is also punctuated with joyful laughter. Well, I think, that seems strange, but then it does take two wings to fly.

I ask Anita, "All this is about water supply?"

She replies, "It is not really about water. It is tribal and about fear of the future. We call it self-determination, even though we know that's a fantasy. You might have to decide whether you are with us or them."

I say, "To me 'us or them' sounds like fighting words."

"Well, we are more lovers than fighters around here. But you can decide for yourself. Come to the meeting at the school. I'll be there."

This sounds almost like she is offering a personal invitation. I feel a hum.

When I get to the meeting that evening, it is well attended with all kinds of people. Some I recognize from the café. Some seem almost normal while others look like they rode out of the woods on bears. Nobody looks the same as anybody else.

After the meeting, I find Anita and ask her to take a walk with me. She says, "There's some place I want to show you, but it is too far to walk."

I feel a deep buzz. Is this really happening? I say, "Well, I guess you get to meet my truck then."

When she climbs in the front seat she says, "This thing has some history."

"Oh yes, I have had it since high school and it was old when I got it. Also, they salt the roads in Illinois, so the floor got corroded. It still works though."

My truck starts right up like it has my back. "Just don't expect much, it goes places, but doesn't provide much comfort on the way."

She directs me through Willits to the outskirts and to what looks like an abandoned industrial site surrounded by a tall wire fence and open fields. The big rusted metal gate is locked.

She says, "I got the key. My dad used to work security after they shut it down."

We step out of the truck and she opens the gate and shuts it behind us.

"What is this place?" I ask.

"This is the old Mendocino Lumber Mill. You can see some of the logs they left after it shut down," she points.

She leads me inside a huge metal mill building with the last remains of sunlight glowing in the high windows. As my eyes adjust, we walk across the open sawdusty floor along a log conveyer, to a set of large old fashioned circular sawmill blades, rusted and hanging from a rack. They range from eight feet diameter or so to less than that.

The fading evening light provides a dimly illuminated backdrop filled with the daydreams of a long history of mill workers. She picks up an old tool hammer from a bench and starts tapping on the blades. They are like gongs, each letting out a deep tone. She plays them in a cascade of notes that echo in the deep space of the mill. Then she plays some old bandsaw blades on the same rack. They add warbly notes to the open space. The sawblade music in the dim light seems to leak magic from an older world. We wait for a few moments as the echoing sounds fade.

"Now, I want to show you something else," she says, even though I have not yet recovered from the gongs that are still ringing in my chest.

We walk back out of the building to a ladder on the side of a tower. She climbs ahead of me, way up the side of an elevated water tower. I follow her up, enjoying the view.

We get to the top and step out onto a slightly tilted conical roof with no railing. She walks to the top and sits down. I sit next to her. Our exposed seats on the top of the water tank provide a hint of danger. The sun has just set and the orange, green, and dark blue sky still illuminates the valley. She gestures saying, "Little Lake Valley."

I look over a flat valley surrounded by steep oak-wooded hills. There is a large wetland of marsh and some open water still reflecting the colors of the sky. There are lights from the town but most of the valley is unlit with just a few sparkles from widespread farms.

"Look to the southeast and you can see Russell and Sally's ranch." I look and look back at her.

After climbing back down, we hold hands on the way to my truck. I am not sure that I can feel the ground.

The next day I file my report on the meeting in Willits.

Fanning the Flames of Discontent

Local Group Organizes to Preserve Blockage of the Eel River Tunnel

By Ryder Jeffers, reporter for the AVA

The accidental blockage of the Eel River Diversion tunnel by a truckload of bovine butt plugs has inspired a local movement to keep the water in the Eel. The local branch of the State of Jefferson organizing committee sponsored a rally at the high school in Willits on Thursday.

Among the headline speakers were notable Mendocino celebrities, June Cleaver, the Ag Commissioner and activist, and Bam Bam Ram, a bald Buddhist monk and band leader of the local Hell's Angels. The Master of Ceremonies was Wavy Gravy, a well-known figure in the county since the seventies.

June Cleaver is a tall athletic woman with a fierce gaze and long curly black hair. She started the meeting by calming the crowd with a look.

In her speech she began by clarifying that she is not the June Cleaver that was the mother of Beaver Cleaver from the 60's sitcom, Leave it to Beaver. Instead, she is the love child of Eldridge Cleaver, convicted rape felon, Black

Panther, minister, author, political refugee, and inventor. In particular, he invented Cleaver Pants, a garment style designed to abundantly house certain parts of the male anatomy in a form-fit codpiece. Although they were never popular with normal-sized men, Eldridge liked to wear them around Oakland looking for likely women. Unfortunately, his sales approach didn't work that well so he never achieved broad market penetration.

This was before Eldridge was a political refugee in Algeria funded by the Viet Cong. Apparently, they got tired of his parties, so they sent him home to California to run for governor. He polled poorly as a Republican.

After Eldridge died, June said she was left with a warehouse full of surplus bi-colored Cleaver Pants in three sizes. She adroitly sold them off to collectors in a lively auction on Ebay along with the warehouse. Her haul from the sale provides her with enough funding to live on a ranch and promote revolutionary activity full time.

She said she has never found anyone that could fill in for her father but that his memory will rise again with the State of Jefferson, where all oppressed peoples will be free to live in abject poverty.

In her long speech the charismatic Ms. Cleaver detailed a new State of Jefferson Declaration of Independence.

"We the People will be free. Free from the domination of wealth and free from the corrupt forces of society. The laws that restrict our freedom are hereby repealed and do not apply within our state.

"We declare our right to seek happiness as citizens under the constitution since we are patriots. We claim our land as the State of Jefferson, named for the man that recognized that all of us are created equal.

"In the tradition of the original Declaration of Independence, the first revolution of the State of Jefferson, and other efforts of free people to be free like the Black Panther Party, the Hells Angels, Buddhism, and the county art commission. We hereby establish our rights. Do not trespass."

I met Bam Bam Ram as he was leaving the rally. Bam Bam is a local leader of the Hells Angels as well as a bald monk dedicated to the Sangha of the City of Ten Thousand Buddhas east of Ukiah. He is short, thin, and ascetic with a shaved head and tattoos snaking up his arms. He wore orange Buddhist robes with a remarkable death's head embroidery on the back.

Bam Bam said that Buddhists at the temple maintain vows of silence, but he was granted an exception by the Lama. "Our spiritual leader signaled me to speak, even though she herself refused to speak in doing so."

He said, "Her holy prominence, Dr. Poon Tang, always keeps her lips tightly pressed to avoid temptation. She leads our Sangha after being elevated to that supreme height with the help of an aerodynamic robe and a good wind just like in that 60's TV show, The Flying Nun. In my case, I usually let my big old chopper do the talking."

We asked Bam Bam about his role in the struggle for the State of Jefferson. He told us, "Struggle is an essential Buddhist goal applied to enlightenment and freedom from desire. In this case we seek freedom from domination by the wealthy water thieves of Sonoma County who apply our waters to feed their intoxicant culture. They are a sad group, drunk on wealth and water. We hope to free them from themselves."

I asked how that fits with his leadership role in the Hell's Angels. "Every revolution needs a charismatic leader, a bard, a martyr, and a military genius," he said. "The Hell's Angels have agreed to embody their roots as rebels against convention. My Angels will provide the spiritual troops for our struggle. I am merely a lens for their militant energies.

"But maybe most important, they help with the music," he said. "Every revolution is also a battle of the bands."

As he roared away on his chopper, his Angels revved their Harleys in a deep-throated echo of his name.

After I write this report, I think this righteous political activity seems typical, just more people protesting government power. When it shows up, government and corporate power usually win, then it turns into the sad vision I saw at the Bad Cowboy Bar in Yreka. Although now I was beginning to feel a little righteous myself. These people out here seem pretty wacky, I think.

Next morning, my mom calls me on my phone.

She says, "Ryder, we need to talk... I got a visit from an FBI agent. They're looking for you."

"What was his name?" I ask.

"I'm not sure. It was Fred something..., Maybe Fred MacMurray?"

"Was it Fred Arally?"

"Yeah," she says, "That's it. He is out front watching right now."

"Mom, he's not an agent. They threw him out. And don't listen to him, he's trying to get at dad through me... Also where did you get my new number?"

"Well, Dad started sending me money, so I went out to see him and got it.""

"He has the guards working for him now. He told me he is handling their retirement accounts and that they always show a profit because he can balance their accounts with other offshore funds. The whole thing sounded like a Ponzi scheme combined with a protection racket to me, so I didn't wanna know about it. Apparently, it's working, because the warden asked him to dinner.

"By the way," she asks, "Do you have a girlfriend yet?"

"Well, I don't know, mom. Maybe she likes me, or maybe she is just friendly. Ask me later."

14

Hell and High Water

Back at the AVA, Bruce Anderson suggests that we write something about the history of the Eel water diversion to provide context. He says, "There's an old geologist that wrote up something on the natural hazards at the dam. You could interview him. I think he lives out on the river."

I set out to hunt down Landon Shore, a retired geologist living out of his van by a bridge on the Eel River. He has been working with Friends of the Eel to assess the diversion and associated Potter Valley Water Project.

On my way to the river, I take the road up Redwood Valley. I pass an elaborate set of temples with numerous stupa and extensive manicured gardens. It stands out from the typical ranch and farms along the way, but seems deserted. I think, maybe they are chanting somewhere or slowly making mandalas with colored sand. I really have no idea what Buddhists do or why.

The road passes the temples, through a tall oak woodland, along a low ridge for a while, then dives into a narrow gulch to the left. The paving deteriorates until it is mostly dirt with occasional paved patches. Then I come to a stream crossing. I get out to look at the water.

Can I cross? The base of the river is cobbly and the water is about a foot deep and clear. So, I go for it. It feels like the stream cools my tires and I proceed almost merrily across. As I reach the other side, the dirt ramp is a little steep. Then partway up, my progress slows and I hear growling and churning from my back wheels. I back up and give it another go, but again I stop, this time with my back wheels lower in the water.

I get out to look at my tires and they are deep in the stream. I start contemplating my options. I have no experience with this kind of stuck.

As I ponder, sitting on the bank while getting more and more desperate, I hear the distant growl of another truck coming behind. It finally pulls up, followed by dust from the road. A bandy-legged man in dusty jeans and a t-shirt gets out.

"Stuck?" he asks.

"Yup."

He wades across the stream. "Hey," he says, "You must be that new reporter. I hear you been out with Anita."

Then he says, "I know, I know, small town OK? Most of us take a special interest in her."

"Why is that," I ask.

"Well, in high school when she showed up as a freshman, all us boys knew it right away. She was a real *bee-hunter*, that is a spirited girl. A couple of years later she started dating. I even took her out once. By the end of the evening, she told me that the boys in our school were too young for our age and that we all said the same stuff. You can imagine I was disappointed."

He continues, "She stayed pretty independent through school but used to hang out a lot with Forrest."

I say, "And now she works as a waitress."

"Oh no," he says, "She started out working there but now she owns the place, the hotel, and the bar next door. Used to be a dump and not worth much. By the way, do you need some help?"

"Yes please, you got a winch?"

"No, but maybe you just need some weight in the back." He steps on the bumper and throws his leg over into the back of my truck and says, "Try it now."

I get in, start up, and the tires catch as I slowly drive my truck up onto the road. I get out and thank him. He says, "No worries, what else was I going to do, you were blocking the road."

I drive on, following a narrow dirt track that leads to a paved road. This takes me through meadows and over a fir-forested ridge down to the Eel River.

I come upon a dusty whitish van parked on the river bank under some huge oaks by an old steel bridge over the river. This must be it. The van is manly, with kayaks on top, two bikes on the back, big studly tires, and four-wheel drive. On the back is a bumper sticker that says, "Cook your kids, good food," which strikes me odd.

I knock on the van door but he isn't there. Then he appears almost immediately from a trail that comes up from the river. He is tall and lean, but old with a scratchy, unshaven face and grey hair. He strolls up to me wearing brown nylon cargo shorts, a t-shirt, boots, and a broad-brimmed Indiana Jones hat. His eyes are a little squinty and he has an indelible tan.

He says, "There is nothing in the van you want, friend."

I tell him, "I know that cause I'm looking for you and you're not in there."

I ask him to sit down on his folding chairs and talk to me while we look at the river. The Eel is rolling by and whooshing past willows and oaks. The sounds of birds and bugs are louder than the leaves in the breeze. The sun sparkles on the ripples.

I start by asking about him. He tells me he is retired but still learning and likes to see stuff for himself. "Are you married? Do you have kids?" I ask.

"Oh my, yes. She'll be along in a minute. And kids too. They are all working as geologists somewhere."

"So, they decided to follow in your footsteps," I say. "That must feel good."

"Well, I think it may have been despite me rather than because of me. It seems that geology is like a genetically-determined personality defect. We can't help ourselves and then we're stuck with it. But they are great kids."

I ask, "Then why do you want to cook them?"

He says, "What?... Oh, you got that from my bumper sticker. The comma on that thing was put on later. I parked my van in downtown Willits while I was getting supplies and somebody came along with a marker pen. I hear that she calls herself the "Comma Bomber." She is probably walking around Willits right now with a permanent marker and a twisted mind."

When I ask him about the water diversion he says, "I spent six months studying the geologic hazards, I read every publication and did some field work. I even submitted my report to the feds and the state.

"I got some help from a fisheries biologist I know, Sal Manley. He told me how early-on the diversion sucked down a lot of salmon that got ground up in the power plant and turned the water green, accidently providing fertilizer for the farmers in Potter Valley." (Editor's note: If you are uncomfortable hearing stories about fish genocide, you should move to Florida, where they keep themselves safe from uncomfortable truths. On the other hand, if you are a salmon, you should sue for reparations.)

Landon tells me, "The history of this project is a long list of decisions bad enough that they are almost funny. I didn't make any of this story up."

I summarize his comments about the project in an article for the AVA.

Fanning the Flames of Discontent

The Tragi-Comedy of The Potter Valley Project

By Ryder Jeffers, reporter for the AVA

Once upon a time, a wealthy San Franciscan, W. "Billy" Van Arsdale, realized that the Eel River was 475 feet higher than the Russian River across a single ridge near Potter Valley. He got the brilliant idea to install a power and irrigation project by diverting the Eel into a mile long tunnel through the ridge that separates it from the Russian. There is no telling how he stole the water rights for it.

The Van Arsdale diversion tunnel shows up on a map of the project that follows this report. The tunnel is now unnaturally blocked by cow suppositories.

Like many brilliant ideas, Billy didn't think it all the way through. Within a few years of constructing the diversion in 1908, they realized that there wasn't enough water in the Eel in the summer and fall to sustain the plant. (Ouch.)

So, the obvious answer was to build a reservoir upstream on the Eel to sustain late summer flows. So in 1922, they set the Scott Dam on an active fault, below a moving landslide, and with the foundation in old landslide deposits. (Whoops.)

They didn't know much about the geology around here back then and decided to build the dam across a narrow section of Gravely Valley so they could buttress on a "bedrock pinnacle" on the other side of the valley.

During construction, with the dam halfway across the valley, high water flow from a storm careened around the end of the unfinished dam. That flood washed out and broke up the bedrock pinnacle. Apparently, it was just a big loose rock in the hillside. (Uh oh.)

After that they decided to turn the dam at a thirty-two-degree angle and complete it to another bedrock pinnacle instead. (What, again?)

Then right after they filled the dam, it started leaking on that same side. (Oh no.) So, they went up and pumped concrete in the ground until it seemed to stop. (Whew.)

Within a few years, in 1928, the Saint Francis Dam in southern California washed out due to a foundation on an active fault and old landslide. (Hmmm.) This was the largest engineering disaster in the history of California. The death toll was reported as 415 people plus an unknown number of Mexicans. (Nobody had bothered to count the population of a small town that was entirely washed away).

Despite the raft of bad decisions and the near miss of disaster from the Potter Valley project in the past, the future history may be just as comical.

Currently the group planning the future of the project intends to both save the water supply into the

Russian and remove the Scott Dam. Their clearly conflicting goals show that they have a lot of work ahead. Neither PGE nor this group has ever removed a dam at this scale.

Meanwhile, the dam is unstable. In the worst-case earthquake, it fails. Also, the spillway is rated to just barely manage flows of a 100-year storm, but nobody knows what that is anymore. With climate change it will be worse than ever. So, the dam is an accident waiting to happen.

If it comes down, a torrent of water, mud, and fragments of dam will come barreling down the canyon like hell and high water at the same time.

While they are fighting about water supply from the dam, the best thing for the river would be to replace some of the spawning gravel that has been blocked by the dam and use the still available dam water to make sure the flows are high enough during migration for vulnerable salmonid fish populations. That way the habitat of the river below the dam can recover to the point that it might survive a dam disaster or even dam removal.

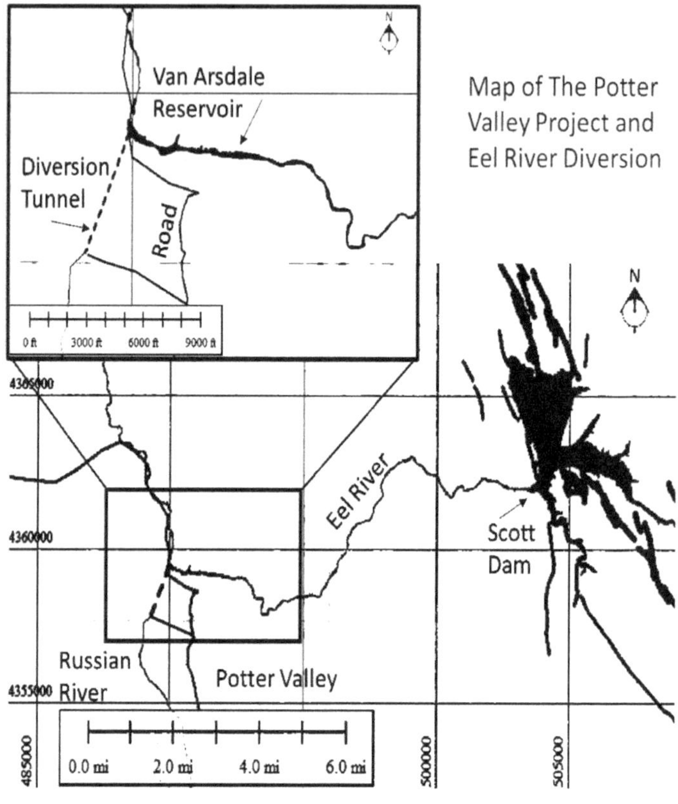

During the interview I wonder why, with this knowledge, Mr. Shore has his van parked downstream of the dam. He says, "That is exactly why I live here. I want to see it when the natural order is restored. But don't worry, I got kayaks."

Before I leave, I tell him, "Thanks for the interview. I like this stuff, maybe I should become a geologist."

He replies, "You can do that. We have a low bar. Just be curious about the earth and then follow up on your questions. There is plenty of stuff that will be coming at us soon. So, watch and learn…. The tricky part, of course, is getting paid for it."

After this article gets published in the AVA, local disaster groupies start buying kayaks that they can throw into their pick-up trucks so they can get out there when the dam breaks. There is nothing like the image of giant fragments of a concrete dam tumbling in a thunderous whitewater flood with other debris to spark imaginations and the latent death wish of a young male audience.

15

Ba-Boom

The revolution is then further inspired by another unfortunate accident…and another lead from Gil Teeman.

I stop by the Sheriff's Office again. He says, "I got a call from some guy from the FBI looking for you. What's that about?"

I cringe and think, how did he find me? He must have tracked that phone call. I tell the sheriff, "Ex-Agent Arally is harassing me about stuff I already told him that I don't know."

"Well," the sheriff says, "I told him I would ask around, but then I checked him out. The FBI told me he doesn't work there anymore."

I wonder if Arally knows where I am staying. It shouldn't be too hard to find me considering I am new in town. I will have to watch my back. I am anxious that he could expose the flagrant lies in my resume.

Would the authentic people I have been meeting in Mendocino be OK with the fraud I brought with me?

To quickly change the subject, I ask the sheriff about the button on his shirt that says "Beware Boomers."

Thinking about my professors back in Illinois, I agree with him, "How did boomers become so clueless? They messed stuff up and can't agree how to fix it. They should just get out of the way."

Sheriff Teeman responds. "Oh, this badge isn't about old guy politics. After all, I am that kind of boomer too and we are underappreciated by the young. We made up lots of great stuff like environmentalism and smoothies, not to mention rock and roll. Perhaps our greatest achievement was to turn the country from the war in Vietnam to the Summer of Love. On the other hand, we also coated the world in plastic, so not all good. But no, this badge isn't about politics, it is actually a warning about extreme flatulence."

"What?"

"Oh yes, most people accidentally fart or sputter, but in my case, I produce well-timed and delicately crafted boomers. It takes discipline to eat a full flatulogenic diet and then hold it for just the right moment. My wife almost divorced me before I achieved control.

"Now I never have accidents, instead they are free speech. Everybody on any side of any issue is united in disagreement with my statements, but they don't wait around to argue about it. I am inspiring them to find togetherness, somewhere else."

I step back. This seems oddly refreshing despite the subject. I almost reach for my back pocket to pump out my solidarity, but I had left my fart cushion in the truck.

Gil continues, "I am well known as a flatulist." Pointing to a statue on a shelf behind his desk he says, "I got this award in our latest competition, in the singing division.

We have an annual event in honor of the original master, Henri Pujols, the first performing flatulist. He was a leading act at the Moulin Rouge in Paris in the eighteenth century for a couple of years. He invented the Pujol Manuever. It involves a combination of kegel flexing and sphincter control to get adequate air intake. Think of it like breath control.

"We call our gathering "Roaring Thunder" because of our unique mode of applause. We hold "Thunder" in a group campsite at the beach because the onshore breeze keeps the air fresh.

"We always have a good time. There is a lot of carrying on and fart jokes. Unfortunately, last summer we got socked in by a bad-ass fog. It got so thick we could hardly see."

I ask myself, is a good ass-fog even possible?

Then I say to the sheriff, "That much farting seems excessive. No wonder you fogged up."

He replies, "It may be excessive, but we think of it more as being anal expressive. On the other hand, we also recognize that cleanliness is paramount. So, we have rules about unintended content.

"We are all trained performers," he continues. "We didn't let that fog stop us. We figured out who was performing by the smell. In fact, our smells have become part of our performance. We have been working that into our preparations so that now our diets are like trade secrets.

"All of us know to avoid sulfur-rich food like broccoli and red meat to limit the bad smell. But I have gone beyond that and developed a unique blend of probiotics, carefully bred to suggest the fragrance of freshly baked bread. I plan to market my probiotics under the name Tailwind® with the tag-line "Let it Fly." They give a whole new meaning to the term fartilicious."

Then he changes the subject to tell me to get my poorly-trained ass out to Philo. He says "I'm not sure what happened out there but it might be another boys-gone-wild event with homemade fireworks. There are a few guys I know who have a long-term fascination with blowing shit up. I knew them in high school. It is a wonder that we lived through it. But, the only report I have so far also said something about a cow. We never went that far before."

This cow shit just got real.

Fanning the Flames of Discontent

Cow Explodes in Philo

By Ryder Jeffers, reporter for the AVA

A man died in Philo yesterday in an explosion triggered by embers from a lit "cigarette." According to the police report, they arrived on the scene to find his distraught partner, Windtree (no last name), moaning incoherently about Bud Cutler. She pointed to the barn and babbled something about cows and an explosion. The barn was blown out at one end and cow and human remains were scattered in the yard.

The report described the debris as wood fragments, blood, and guts. When asked how they identified the victim, a police representative said "The human victim was identified from his head. It landed in an orchard downhill from the barn. We often find cranial projectiles in this type of incident."

On our way to the scene, AVA interviewed Calum Potter, one of Bud's close friends from high school. Calum told us, "Bud Cutler was a libertarian hippie child with a marijuana license and a handgun. He always came in here wearing a Che Guevara hat and one of those tie-dyed shirts with pockets that his mom makes to sell in the Boonville store. He raises cattle and pot out north of Philo. That boy was a genius and way too smart for his own good. We knew him as Leonardo Duh Philo."

When challenged on whether the reference to Da Vinci was an exaggeration, Calum told us of one of their escapades from high school.

"We used to raid Hagarty's apple orchard on the way home from school every day. We liked to climb their banana apple tree. We loved eating creamy apples way up in the leafy branches and thought nobody knew, despite our giggling and the pile of apple cores next to the trunk.

"Anyway, we were down at the store one day and crawled up behind Mrs. Hagerty at the check-stand to look up her skirt. She took it kinda personal and started yelling. The next thing you know, Old Mr. Hagerty put up a bobwire (sic) fence around their orchard. He yelled 'That'll teach you little perverts!' at us as we walked by the next day.

"Bud took that a bit contrary. The next week he invited me to see what he was making in his barn. He had fixed an old irrigation pipe up at an angle sticking out the hay door of the barn and had five farm-size air pump pest sprayers plumbed up in a battery to feed a giant air cannon pointed directly at Hagerty's. He even painted along the barrel announcing that it was a Cutler Squirrel Cannon®. Bud said 'Hagerty won't know what hit him. Once I start firing squirrels into his trees, he will never see another apple without a bite in it.'

"I asked him how he figured on squirrels and he said, 'Cats squirm too much in flight, so they don't glide well.'

"When I suggested that the squirrels might end up smashed against tree branches or the ground, he had that figured too. 'Don't worry, I aim above the trees and my mom made me a bunch of little parachutes. At first, she objected when she thought I was going to test it out on her cat again. But when I told her that NASA uses monkeys for their work, she calmed down and got on board.'

"Then Bud said, 'Let's try it out. I am ready for a test shot.' He put on an oven mitt, reached into a barrel, and pulled out a squirrel that was squirming, spitting, and viciously clawing. 'I'll just tie on his little parachute while you get the sprayers pumped up.' After loading the squirrel into a breach door on the pipe, he stood back and said, 'Climb up to the loft and report on the landing zone.'

"Then FWWUMP! The cannon let loose.

"That, my friend," Callum told me, "Is natural military genius, just like Da Vinci."

By the time your reporter arrived at the Bud's farm and met his wife, Windtree, she had calmed down. "He read those articles in your newspaper about that cattle sickness and the one on the crash up at Van Arsdale. Them's what started it. He thought for a couple of days and then told me that plugging up the tunnel with suppositories was just a beginning. He said he had a better idea." Then she pointed out back and said "Now look at the barn…. And, by the way, his real first name is Quentin."

We asked for her story on what happened and she told us, "After he got an idea in his head, he was hard to stop. Right after he told me about his idea he left for the store. He got back with several jars of Kaopectate and some surgical supplies, and the next thing I know I see him chasing one his cows across the field with a piece of plastic tubing and a funnel."

She said, "Quentin should have been an inventor; he just ended up stuck in the woods with an overactive imagination. He always loved to experiment with stuff and he kept at it. Then he would come back with filthy overalls 'cause one of his experiments led to a blow-out. I made him hose down out in the yard. That man was persistent but not really all that good with animals.

"I knew he was in trouble when I caught him studying up on the internet about how to design a shaped charge. I think he planned to round up a formation of gassed-up cows with one that was rigged with primer cord. He told me that he was going to lead them in glorious battle. Then he stood up and left the room with a fire in his eyes and that's the last time I saw him alive."

Obituary: Quentin Cutler, survived by his partner, Windtree, his dog Wegner, and a herd of nervous looking cows. He is also mourned by his mother, who still lives in the woods somewhere north of Boonville.

After I get this report into the paper, I start feeling better about myself. This is working. Contemplating my apparent success, I notice that at least some of it is coming from the delightful and diverse personalities around me.

I am hanging out at my usual table at the café when I am approached by a rough man with blond dreads wearing a uniform with a Calfire badge. His long rasta-knotted hair hangs over his shoulders and down his back and behind his knees like he never cut it. His eyes sparkle from under wispy eyebrows.

"Hey," he says, "My name's Forrest, Forrest Byrne."

"Right," I say, "I heard you were good friends with Anita."

"Not just friends… Anyway, I read your report about Bud and his squirrel cannons. I can verify that story. I was there."

"Really," I reply.

"Yeah, I was out driving in my pick-up truck doing the laundry in the bed and putting my buddy's kid to sleep in the back seat when I first heard that squirrel cannon."

"What? Wait a minute," I say confused. "You were washing your clothes in a pickup truck?"

"Oh yeah, we couldn't always get into town to do laundry so we would get naked and load up all our clothes and some soapy water in a 55-gallon drum in the back of a pick-up. Drive it around for a while on back roads to agitate and you can get the wash done and put the kid to sleep while you're driving."

"So how did you know the sound was from a squirrel cannon?"

"I didn't then. But I was out at our grow the next day when we got raided by cartel hoods. They showed up in black SUVs and shot off some guns. Our clothes hadn't dried, but we had our shoes on so we ran up the canyon. I climbed a big fir tree to see what was happening and they were stuffing our crop into the backs of their trucks. I had a cell phone so I called the sheriff."

"Weren't you worried about getting busted?"

"Nah, this is Mendo man. Pot is free speech here. Besides we were just making a living and my buddies are kin to the sheriff. Meanwhile, armed robbery is something else. After the deputies hauled those creeps away, they kept our crop. I guess they don't get paid much.

"After that we figured we needed protection of our own so when we found out about his cannon, we got Bud to build us some artillery. We used to fire off a few squirrels as practice when we got buzzed after a hard day on the grow. Some of those little squirrels were thrill-seekers. They would come back for more with their parachutes still tied on.

"That was back when pot sold for $5000 a pound. After it got legalized, the price dropped and we all had to get jobs. I had plenty of experience taking out brush and got a job clearing fuel breaks for Calfire. They liked me and now I work as a spotter. I climb up trees, look for smoke, and direct the crews."

He steps back and walks over to the counter to talk with Anita. They tilt their heads together and laugh quietly. I think, what is going on? Jealousy rises, my eyes showing a bit of green for no good reason. I try to hold my composure.

After he leaves, I go ask Anita about boyfriends. I realize she must know plenty of other men. Unfortunately, I come across a little aggressive. I am not very experienced with caring for people, since my most affectionate moments have been focused on a pick-up truck.

"Just like a man," she says. "Can't you think outside your own mind? Just go away."

This is a crisis. My hopes and emerging thoughts of a joyful relationship after all those teenage fantasies are struck down. Maybe I am just one of many. I have a bout with anxiety.

Then I think, on the other hand, she called me a man. I try that on for size.

15

The Peaceful Revolution

The emergence of Bud Cutler as a martyr enflames the popular uprising with the help of plenty more Free Speech. In his columns Bruce points out that the local history of revolution was not only successful but also mostly peaceful. His examples include the California Bear Flag Revolt where the combatants resolved the initial dispute by sharing brandy with General Vallejo in his parlor and the only California Civil War battle that ended up as a drinking contest at the Washoe House Bar between Petaluma and Santa Rosa. Clearly revolution does not require a lot of violence around here.

My editor writes, "Ever since the local Pomo Indians greeted Sir Francis Drake with gifts and speeches, we have been hospitable to change."

After Bud's death and the reports of his cow brigade plan in the AVA, along with Bruce's suggestion that free speech, broadly defined, might be enough, the entire community gets on board, including the sheriff, the county supervisors, and the art commission. The

Buddhist community nods peacefully in agreement. Meanwhile, the State of Jefferson Committee with the help of the Hell's Angels organizes occupation of the entrance to the plugged tunnel to discourage the maintenance crews from PG&E.

I hear about an organizing meeting from Anita, who apparently holds a position of respect in the community. She tells me that the initial enthusiasm to keep the water in the Eel led to a tactical discussion about weaponry. Surprisingly, the idea to leave guns at home came from rank and file in the Hells Angels. "If you aren't going to use them, don't bring 'em." One of the State of Jefferson cadre added, "Our goal is revolution, not war."

Anita tells me, "We all looked each other in the eye and decided to commit to our neighbors instead of internet chat groups. We bonded over the revelation that we are a community. As usual, all that love was boosted by shared intoxicants."

16

God Shares

While local Mendocino people are rising to protect the waters of the Eel, the blockage of the water diversion is not popular down south. At The AVA, we read about rumblings in the nether regions of the north coast in their regional newspaper, The Press Demagogue.

The paper reports that a wealthy conspiracy of vineyard owners, brewers, and golfers organized and had an angry meeting about the stoppage of water diversions into the Russian River. In the meeting they shouted at each other and every one of them knew exactly what to do, even though all their opinions differed. Local law enforcement showed up to observe, but then left since the crowd seemed harmless.

After I read about the meetings, I decide to head down south to investigate. I need to get out of town to avoid Fred Arally, but I also feel inspired by him to go undercover.

I call up a few winery owners under the guise of seeking ad commitments for the AVA. Very few call me back, that is to say, one calls me back. I wonder what makes him want to talk to me. Later I found it hard to shut him up.

I interview Godfrey Banks in his office. He is the owner of the 666 Geyserville Road Winery and Pastelleria. He is short and moderately round and wearing rich casual. His hair is slick and dark over a high, pale forehead and has a copy of The Art of War by Sun Tzu on his desk. He is wearing an odd puffy dark grey coat, even on a warm day, and sits in an elaborate high-backed chair behind a bare modern glass desk. The light streams in from tall stained-glass windows behind him. The windows show a cherubic angel ascending to the light.

He greets me with, "My name is Godfrey, but you can call me God, … God Banks."

"Really," I say sarcastically. "Well, God, you have been asleep at the wheel lately. Things in this world are pretty messed up. What have you been doing, contemplating your navel?"

He responds exuberantly by lifting his shirt, "No navel!"

"So, have you been engaging in medical self-mutilation in order to resemble your nickname?" I spit.

Unfazed by my cynicism he pronounces, "Not at all, I don't need to compare myself to other deities, after all, I'm rich."

I reply, " But you must have heard the proverb about wealth, the camel, the eye of the needle, and heaven, right?"

He says, "Oh they made that up to encourage people to give all their money to the church. Then they comfort them in poverty by saying that Jesus was poor too. I have a lot more money than that guy. Meanwhile I plan to make a heaven for the wealthy. It will be a great investment, but with no returns."

"Isn't there a reason why the 10,000 virgins in the Islamic afterlife are still virgins," I say. "Life on a cloud seems fine until you realize what you have to give up."

He laughs, "Oh yeah, but we are not going there anytime soon. A heaven designed for the wealthy is only the long-term part of my proposal. I have shorter-term plans as well.

"I bought the technology that uses transfusions of young blood to extend life. Better than that, injection of baby blood has been proven to make the old become young again. It works for mice in scientific tests and it works for me. I can show you."

He lifts his shirt again and points past his smooth pink belly to a couple of plastic tubes coming out of his shaved left underarm. "You must be aware that research labs are already using stem cells to grow human body part replacements. My engineers went beyond that to build a replica of the entire human circulatory system. This surgical tubing leads from my veins to a specially-designed succubus sown into the lining of my coat. It is a fully-functional, genetically-engineered, living, infantile human circulatory system with an inner layer of bone marrow. It generates new baby blood 24-7. The parts for this thing were grown in my stem-cell lab in the Bay Area. It's now in my coat.

"I need to get a new one grown every several years, but it is better than plugging into a baby pig with a modified blood type carried around in a backpack. Carrying all that weight got tiring," he says. "Lucky I was able to sell them off for parts."

I ask, "You carried around a piglet in a backpack as a source of baby blood?"

God replies, "Well, I tried baby monkeys, but they kept throwing shit around." He unconsciously combs his slick hair back with his hand. "That became unsanitary."

I notice his eyes. When talking about his coat, his irises show white all the way around. Then I look at his coat. It is dark grey and unlike any coats I ever saw in Chicago. I notice the logo low on one side. It says, "The Dorian Grey®."

He continues, "In order to skirt FDA regs. I can't sell coats, but if you own the process, you can apply it to yourself, no problem. So instead, I can sell you shares. You can be an owner too."

I notice a slight fog rising in the room. I look around and down but it is hard to tell. When I look up again a new light is shining from behind me. The light glints off his shiny forehead and refracts in the fog, creating beams of light, radiating from his head. At first, I think the halo might be accidental but then the light turns from white to gold and the rays start to rotate. I wonder who designs his special effects.

He continues, "In addition to keeping my body young, I am concerned about keeping my brain young too. I was taking psychedelics to maintain brain plasticity. Therapeutic psychedelics are already a cutting-edge treatment for PTSD. I was among the first to use them systematically for enhancement of a healthy brain. Unfortunately, they worked too well and ended up giving me a toddler brain to go with the young blood.... Then I almost lost my driver's license.

"I love driving my car, so I switched to transcranial magnetic brain stimulation which also liberates brain plasticity and is easier to control. Magnetic brain stimulation has been successful in treating depression. It usually happens in a clinic with electrical equipment hooked up to an electrode helmet. That is cumbersome, so I got the clinical version re-designed as a wearable device. We fit our version into a beret and glasses so I also look smart.

"When I am wearing them, I can tune the frequency and wave interference on that thing until it feels like I am getting a Brain Boner®. Playing with the controls a bit can blow your mind. Everyone will want one. My focus group tells me that "Brain Boner" sounds too much like "bone brain" so I am still working on the marketing."

Then he tells me, "But life extension and brain plasticity are just the short-term part of my plan. To make real money, I go beyond tech all the way to religion.

"Let me give you some background. Historically, Christianity celebrated poverty and told people to give what they had to the church. But then Norman Vincent Peale and Oral Robertson changed religion so it was holy to get rich first, then give it to the church. They call it the Prosperity Gospel.

"I am transcending the Prosperity Gospel with an IPO that I call God Shares. My IPO forges the final link between the Prosperity Gospel and the stock market. Instead of accepting donations, I can sell you a piece of the action along with a place in heaven. The youth extension and brain plasticity are just the tech components."

Reflecting on his sales pitch, It seems to me that bone brain might be one of the long-term neurological impacts from his self-experimentation. On the other hand, if I had any money, I would invest.

Exhausted by Godfreys complicated technology, grandiosity, and exhibitionism, I remember my dad. Although he was always looking for easy riches, he never had much success outside of prison. Not like this guy. It certainly seems that Godfrey is just as deluded as my father, maybe more so. Was it just that

Godfrey got lucky? Are capitalists just a bunch of psychopaths that only seem smart because they randomly pick a lucky delusion and have the money to hire good engineers? Meanwhile, this guy makes my new friends in Mendocino seem normal.

I turn the conversation to advertising.

"We have pretty good circulation up in Mendocino too," I say. "The AVA is the premier publication north of Santa Rosa. Not to mention our online readership. Our literary content even outshines the Register Guard all the way up in Eugene. So, if you want to get your story out up north, there is nothing better than the Anderson Valley Advertiser."

I surprise myself with my own enthusiasm. It is out of character. I love my new job. I am not sure when this happened, but caution seems to have fled after years of disappointment. Am I also deluded? Do I care? In any case I am looking forward to getting lucky.

My pitch is successful in selling a full-page ad. Godfrey says, "Why not?" and I don't respond with reasons.

Then, after my mention of Mendocino, he brings up water supply for vineyard operations.

"That water going into the Russian River is ours and nobody can take it from us," he says. "There is a rabble up there trying to steal it and I need to resolve that in my favor. But I didn't get wealthy by spending my own money, so I sold the movie rights first and then formed a cheap militia from a homeless encampment along the river behind my vineyard. I am paying them in surplus wine, snack food, and free t-shirts that promise a better life. Plus, I am tired of their trash. They are rallying out at the fairgrounds right now. Meanwhile I get to keep most of the movie money. That is my kind of capitalism," he says.

"My engineers are also making up something special that might solve some of my water problems. Do you want to take a look?"

I say, "Ohh yes. Do you have a secret basement lab or what?"

God stands up with a slight grin, steps down from the platform under his chair and a cheerfully leads me out of his office and down the hallway. We get to a white steel door that says "Authorized Personnel" which he unlocks with a thumbprint. We descend a long white concrete stairway lit by bare bulbs. The stairway is long enough that I look back more than once, wondering where this will end. We must be underground by the time we get to another locked door.

God opens the door at the bottom and we step into a large brightly lit room with various work stations and a variety of large tools, equipment, benches, and cabinets with parts of all types. Several people are working on machining and soldering at different stations. In the middle of the room stands a tall black man. He turns.

"Dr. Osgood!" I exclaim in surprise and shock. "What are you doing here?"

"Hello Ryder," Charles replies, "They read my thesis on nanobubble formation and asked me to come out and develop a treatment for sparkling wine. Nanobubbles are just very tiny bubbles that can stay in suspension, so they don't come out on the glass. I showed them how to make nanobubbles inside their process and we came out with a distinctive silky taste in wine that they liked. Then Godfrey here hired me full time."

I look across at Godfrey. God says, "We call it The Silk®. The unique feel of that wine has created a real buzz in the market. The fact that it must be served within a couple of weeks has ironically increased demand." Looking at Dr. Osgood he says, "This man is brilliant as well as beautiful."

Charles goes on, "Now, I am working on another project. Come on over here, I'll show you." We walk to the far end of the shop where a large cylindrical device lies on a work table. Charles proudly gestures to the device.

"Godfrey tells me they have problems with plugged pipes. So, I am working on a device to clean them out. I already have a prototype so this is our first production model. These tools are based on 12-inch diameter tubing. They have a swivel head with teeth and an internal turbine to spin the head from the water flow. It works like a directional drilling tool on an oil rig. The water flow spins the head then spits out of the head from a series of nozzles. We should be able to drill through the sludge in plugged winery pipelines and circulate it out with the water flow.

"After reading about him in the AVA, I contracted Conner Rhia to design turbulators for the nozzles to take advantage of vortex cutting action. "I call my device "The Enema®." It's the enemy of sludge."

I look at him a little stunned. I am also surprised about the market penetration of the AVA.

Charles says, "I was pleased when I saw your byline. I was worried after what happened back in Chicago. Are you out here to make a new start?"

I reply, "I am starting over. But there is an ex-FBI agent looking for me. Remember him from school that day?"

"Oh you mean the guy on the steps? Well, keep your head down. He seemed pretty nasty."

Charles and I hug. "It's great to see you," I say. "We need to get together."

The he tells me that he has to get back to work. "We are about to start a durability test on my new tool."

Meanwhile, after hearing about God's homeless mercenaries, I have another stop planned, out at the fairgrounds.

On my way to my truck, I notice a sleek-looking brushed stainless-steel car in a reserved parking space in front of the winery. I think, oh my god, he has a Delorean.

17

The Round-Up

I head over to the Sonoma County fairgrounds to check out God's homeless mercenary army. I park on Santa Rosa city streets and cross to the fairgrounds on foot.

As I near the huge blocked-off county fair parking lot I hear a commotion. There is a large crowd circling around in a parade, riding on golf carts festooned with colorful banners. They are wearing black t-shirts with a "God Shares" logo. The free wine must have encouraged attendance because there is a lot of shouting and singing going on, not to mention a few bottles clinking around in the back of golf carts.

I take pictures of the frantic spinning parade with my phone and immediately send a copy to Bruce with an intelligence brief from my undercover work with Godfrey. I ask him, "Can you believe this?" under the photo.

In the background of my photo there are some big trucks in front of the fair buildings with cloth banners hanging from the beds. The circling carts in front stir up a vortex mushroom of dust that rises over the scene. I pull out my phone again to get another shot.

Then I hear a loud "No photos" from behind me. I turn around. He is big, carrying a police-style baton and a scowl. He walks up to me with his long frizzy hair tied back in a grey pony tail. He looks like a brutish British bobby on a bad hair day. His lips turn down and his yellowish teeth show. The tattoo on his bicep says, "Mom" pierced by a cupid's arrow. I notice the t-shirt label blazoned across his broad chest, it says, "Security God."

I say, "It's OK, I'm a journalist."

"I don't care who you think you are," he says. "This is a private event. No photos. So, either erase them or I'll take your phone."

"You can't take my phone," I challenge.

"Is that right," he says slapping his baton on his hand.

I think about it a moment and then comply, showing him each photo and then deleting it.

Later, as I am walking back to my truck, a muddled chant starts rising from the mercenary army. Security God is standing on a platform in front of the trucks. He has a megaphone. I listen more closely. What is he chanting? I chuckle when I hear the crowd yelling with him, "Save the Russians, Save the Russians!" I think, he's right, they probably need it.

The next day, God sends me his ad copy. it reminds me of my dad selling recent lava flows on an active volcano to shut-ins with too much extra money.

When Bruce sees the ad, he exclaims, "You sold an ad!"

"Yes, and I took cash. He offered me two for one in shares instead, but I thought they couldn't be worth much if he was giving them away cheap. He probably just prints them up as needed."

"And what is with that photo you sent?" He asks.

"I am not sure, but I get the feeling that they are heading to Van Arsdale."

Bruce says, "If they are coming, we better get ready. Ms. Cleaver and the leadership team are already getting prepared for that after I forwarded your note. We had a strategy session last night."

Then I tell Bruce more about Godfrey and his IPO. Bruce responds with, "Nobody is going to send that wacko their hard-earned money."

I tell him, "Have you not been reading the news? Lies are currency and the more of a fake news world you can build around you, the more money people send. Unfortunately for many in this world, lies are more believable as they get more elaborately fake. It is not about fact; it is more whether you want to believe. He just has to tell his lies faster than they can think up the truth. And many people would rather not spend their time engaged in critical thinking. It's hard work."

18

Flying Squirrels

Bruce tells me to skip writing about God for now and report on a demonstration planned for the next afternoon at the Van Arsdale Reservoir. "We need to get out the word. Plus, they will need some supplies. After your intelligence report from down south, we expect opposition at the site. I printed up some posters for the event last night at AVA."

I load the posters up behind my passenger seat.

On my way out of town on my way to Van Arsdale, I pass Forrest Byrne on the side of the road with the hood on his pick-up propped up. I stop to help and he tells me that he blew a gasket and asks for a ride out to Van Arsdale.

As he tells me that he is now an officer of the revolution, a muffled sound of determined squeaks comes from a barrel in the back of his truck.

"What is that?" I ask.

He says, "Ammunition" and lifts the top of the barrel. "These guys are my side gig."

The barrel is full of squirrels crawling over each other and chirping. I notice that they have on sparkly suits.

I ask where he got the squirrels. Forrest says, "These guys are professionals. They are second and third generation from my original team that started out as cannon fodder at our pot farm. These guys all grew up in military families. I call them Squirrel Team Six®.

"They have a warrior culture. The little ones start early, jumping from tree limbs and screeching, like kids everywhere. When they are coming of age, they go on a team vision quest into the woods where they work together to scare the shit out of hunters.

"It is a real test because the hunters have guns. They usually miss the first squirrel or two and by then it is too late. The squirrel team learns evasive maneuvers on the fly under live fire. Both squirrels and hunters enjoy the event. By the time the squirrels are big enough for the cannons, they already have the skills and mindset.

"The hunters enjoy the test because they get to shoot their guns. Then, after they get overwhelmed by the squirrels, we serve free beer. By the end of the night, they are all friends. We hand out *squirrel bacon* t-shirts to the hunters. *Squirrel bacon* is *Boontling* for roadkill. They love that.

"We hire out Squirrel Team Six® to protect pot grows. Once the cartel guys are attacked by flying squirrels, they tend to look elsewhere to raid pot farms. We have chased them entirely out of the county. Our team makes enough on that work that we could afford an exercise-weight room at my house." Looking again, I notice that the squirrels seem pretty buff and some have pronounced biceps.

The biggest squirrel looks directly at me and slowly smiles. His teeth have been sharpened to points. Forrest says, "That's our squad leader, Rocky II. We figure that inciting fear in your enemy is more powerful than actual violence. Anyway, it seems to work." Then the other squirrels smile too. I step back.

Forrest continues, "Meanwhile the parachutes kept getting tangled so we upgraded to squirrel flight suits, so now we channel Rocky, The Flying Squirrel."

I can see that the sparkly flight suits on the squirrels have wings that stretch between the front and back legs. I say, "The sparkles make them look patriotic."

Forrest says, "They also dazzle the eye. The short delay when you are wondering what the hell is coming at you can be enough for the squirrels to reach their targets. I am including the suit design in my patent app.

"By the way, Windtree has signed on with my team. She cleaned out that wreck that used to be a barn so we could use the ruins as a work space. She and Bud's mom are on the patent."

Looking into the barrel, Forrest says. "Chirp, chirpity, click-click." The squirrels immediately quiet and snuggle down into the barrel. As he replaces the top, Forrest tells me, "They will stay quiet on the drive. They are used to road travel."

"Were you just talking to them?" I ask.

"Not really, I only know a few phrases. If I need to provide detail, I use cowboy talk. They learned cowboy by watching John Wayne movies back at the house. I'll show you, listen to this."

Forrest then stands with his legs apart facing the barrel and intones with a drawl, "Never apologize partner, it's a weakness." The chirping in the barrel goes wild.

We shift the barrel from his truck to mine. As we head out to Van Arsdale, Forrest talks to me about targeting and glide path strategies. He describes their high-low blitz technique. "After that, the opposition is usually in full flight or waddling around with a load in their panties."

When we get to Van Arsdale, Forrest shows me his cannon assembly team already onsite. Some of the irrigation pipe is still stacked to one side. A crew is using a block and tackle to haul one into position. There are air pumps piled up under an oak tree. Forrest starts striding around exhorting the crew.

"Progress," he says, "Good progress."

His voice rises in command, "Now let's get another crew set with ropes and pulleys. We can use these trees as support." The placement of the cannons behind a line of trees on the ridge makes it clear that somebody has a battle strategy in mind.

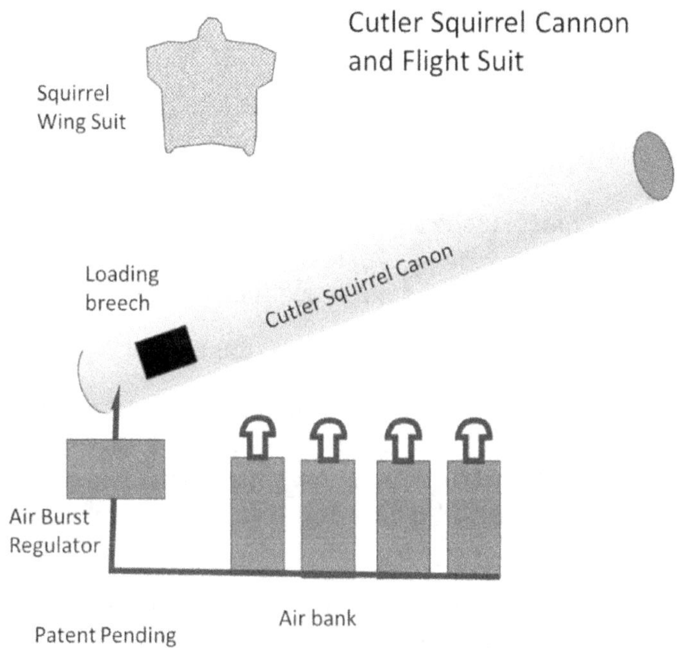

My phone rings and I step away. I get a call from Russell Brand, "Ryder, I need your help," he says. I drop off the banners and the barrel and turn my truck around to head up to Willits. It turns out Russell needs to move his herd. I am excited all the way there.

19

The Cattle Drive

I meet Russell at his spread southeast of Willits around mid-day. He is dressed to ride with chaps and a rope. He says, "We gotta move these cattle. I need help."

"Where we goin'?" I say, instantly on board.

"I got a call from Ms. Cleaver, she needs them out at Van Arsdale tomorrow. We can take 'em cross-country and bed 'em overnight at a summer pasture we have in the hills."

Russell pulls out a cowboy hat and hands it to me. "Put it on. you'll need it." I am reminded of the shiny plastic star I had back in Chicago.

Russell says, "You need boots with pointy toes for the stirrups but we don't have time for that."

I find Aragorn already saddled in the yard. After mounting, Ms. Brand comes out of the house with a saddlebag. She says, "Tie this on so you two will have something to eat tonight."

Russell says, "The light of my life."

Then we ride through a gate to a large paddock with the herd and start riding back and forth to get them moving. Russell's dogs are helping but stay safely back from the cattle. We head them doggies out a gate at the back of the meadow and up a low ridge.

We spend most of the rest of the day in the dust, riding back and forth to keep the herd together and moving them through open oak woodland. The cows are still spreading diarrhea. One cow is clearly pregnant and is slower than the rest. Russell tells me she may give birth soon, but will be fine. "The walk will do her good."

I find it surprisingly easy but hard and dusty work and reminds me of my childhood.

Late that afternoon we arrive to a broad grassy mountain valley surrounded by oaks and rife with flowers with an old building on one side and a corral.

I ask Russell, "So, is that a bunkhouse?"

He says, "Yes, but rats took that over long ago. And where there's rats, there's snakes. We can bed down over here by this oak and sleep under the stars."

We tie our horses to a post, lay out a couple of bedrolls, and then let the horses out to graze. The sky is treating us to a few lit-up clouds and deepening color.

We sit down to rest and Russell tells me a story about coming up here on a cattle drive when he was a kid.

"My grandpa was all over this country. That first night he took me out, he told me a story about looking for stray cattle on foot. He said he came upon a nest of rattlers. He saw a couple of pairs copulating right there on some rocks. Each one twisting around the other.

"He saw hundreds of snakes around him in that nest. So, he stopped and slowly backed up just like you should. But they started coming after him. He took off and bounded splashing across a stream. The snakes swam in pursuit, thrashing their tails in the water. Most were carried off in the current but one made it across. As Gramps was struggling through the brush on the other side, it struck. Once he saw that snake snagged on his instep, he stomped with his other foot, and saved it for dinner."

Russell starts a fire in an old camp grill. After cooking we sit on a log and eat while watching the cattle in the evening. Russell comments, "Gramps said there are snakes all over here, but don't worry, they won't find your bedroll."

As dusk falls, we climb into bed. I check but no snake. I slide down inside. It's a little chilly, but warms up as my mind quiets down and prepares to dream, finally feeling at home.

Much later, Russell wakes me in the dark with a lantern. I come awake, still bleary. One of the cows is bellowing out in the meadow. Russell says, "That cow has decided to give birth tonight. We need to go out and help or she could have trouble."

I get up, still waking and not thinking yet.

He is carrying a rope and hands me the lantern. "Come on, but watch out for snakes. If you step on one, just jump to the side. They don't react too fast at night."

We are walking out into the meadow and I realize I am only wearing socks. I say, "I need my shoes."

Russell replies, "No time for that."

We get to the cow, who is bellowing like mad and standing splay-footed. Russell says, "You hold the light and I'll tie on." He grabs the rope from around his shoulder, unrolls it, and makes a lasso at one end. Then he walks to the cow. "Come on," he says to me.

I follow. He gets on his knees and puts his hand with the rope and then arm into the back end of the cow. She is already hollering but this encourages her. Russell grunts, "Once I get the feet caught up, you have to help me pull her out, so grab some rope."

His arm goes into the cow up to his shoulder, then he works it, and after a few minutes says, "OK, now start pulling."

I start backing up, holding the rope. Russell takes his arm out of the cow, picks up the rope in front of me, and pulls. I am pulling harder and backing up, slow at first.

Then I step on a snake.

"AAAAK!," I yell and jump, shocked, letting go of the rope.

The cow startles and takes off running and Russell falls and drags along the ground still holding the rope. In the light of the lantern which I still have in a death grip, I see the rope whipping away. Oh no, I think, that wasn't a snake.

Meanwhile Russell is back up, takes the rope, and makes one quick turn around a tree stump. The baby calf yanks out by the momentum of his mom, who abruptly stops and sits down. The baby stands up shaky and wobbles over to mama.

When we get back together, I meekly apologize to Russell for dropping the rope. I say, "I thought it was a snake."

Russell grumps, "There's no snakes out here dummy. They can't eat a cow and don't like getting stomped."

"What about the rats in the bunkhouse and all the copulating you told me about? And you said to not step on them."

"Ohh, those snakes. Well, I admit to twisting you up on that, just like my grandpa did to me. You really don't see snakes much but stories like that are a tradition."

The next day we get up early to round up the herd and drive them down the ridge to Van Arsdale. The new calf is frisky and dancing around while mom lumbers along stoically. It is mostly downhill so it's easy to keep them moving. I need to compensate for screwing up last night and ride Aragorn back and forth around the back of the herd while Russell mostly follows.

After a couple of hours, we are riding behind the herd and Russell tells me, "You got this pretty quick." He looks at me like I am a cowboy instead of a greenhorn.

I reply, "I already lived this life once."

20

The Battle At Van Arsdale

We arrive to a field at the mouth of the diversion tunnel with the herd. There is a crowd of people gathered in a field alongside a small reservoir on the river. The hills behind them are oak woodlands with open grass fields. The sun is bright and the sky has a few clouds.

I recognize some of my new friends, Buzz Mackey, Annie Malls, Conner Rhia, and a few of the regulars from the Boonville Café. Even Banana Whip shows up clutching a beer with his rat-bit hand still festering in a ragged bandage.

I notice that Forrest is being friendly and holding hands with a woman that has blue hair and elaborate make-up. Oh good, I think, one less competitor. On second look, I am stunned that the woman looks just like that evil special agent, Fred Arally. I think he must be undercover.

Fred walks over to me, "I tracked your old phone down, so thanks a lot. Then I found out about your new phone after that call with your mom. So, I followed you again… But now I think I like it here… It feels like I can be me."

Thinking about Rocky the Flying Squirrel, I ask, "I see you're undercover, if are you going as Natasha, where's Boris?"

Fred says, "Maybe I'll be Boris tomorrow, I'm not sure. Nobody out here is going to care. Isn't that great?"

He continues, "I was tracking your phone to get paid off or expose your lies. Then I went out to shake down your dad, and now I'm working for him, so I can let your ass slide.

"He brought me around to a whole new approach to life. I was in a mean state and it has been quite a journey climbing out of that. His joy in living his own lies made me rethink.

"Your dad then asked me to track you down. Once I got out here, meeting people in Mendocino freed me to see that I was living a lie in other ways too." He turns to look adoringly at Forrest. "Some things are more important than money."

I ride over to the talk to the sheriff. When he sees me coming, he waves me over. He is standing next to Bruce Anderson and Whip.

He holds up his phone. "So Ryder, where did you get this photo?"

"Well, Sherriff, I was checking out the gathering of that homeless army down in Sonoma County at the fairgrounds. They seemed more like a group of kids playing on go-karts than anything else. But as you can see from the photo, there were a lot of them. Way more than we have here. It seems like they are planning to come our way."

"Actually," says the sheriff, "I am more interested in these trucks that show up in the background. I asked Whip what he thought."

Whip chimes in, "This truck in the front is clearly a pump truck and the next one back is carrying coiled tubing. I drove rigs like that when I was working on a drilling project at The Geysers. They use the pumps and tubing to stimulate deep steam wells by pumping a big whack of water down the well, hoping it makes the well better."

The sheriff says, "This last flatbed obviously has a couple ATVs, a forklift, and this funny-looking pipe thing. What do you think is going on?"

I look at the photo and think about my trip down south. There is something about the photo. I hesitate. My mind takes a leap. Then I say, "Sherriff, I don't think you are going to like this."

All three look at me. "What?" they say.

"When I was in Dr. Osgood's lab, they had a giant hydroblasting pipe cleaner laid out in their secret basement laboratory. I thought they were going to clean out fermentation sludge from winery pipelines. But maybe they plan to run that thing up the diversion tunnel from the back end using the pump, coiled tubing, and the ATVs to pull Dr. Osgood's pipe cleaner up the tunnel. If they clean out Dr. Rhia's Superswell® plug with that blaster, it's game-over for us."

"Holy shit," says Bruce, "the diversion tunnel is getting an enema!"

"Yeah," I say, "That's what they call it."

Then the sheriff says, "Oh no, they could be launching a two-pronged attack! We are in big trouble. I better make some calls." He walks off, pulling up his phone.

Then events kind of take off. Later I file this report.

Fanning the Flames of Discontent

Ruckus on the River

By Ryder Jeffers, reporter for the AVA

The blockage of the diversion from the Eel to the Russian has led to occupation of the entrance to the diversion tunnel at Van Arsdale by Buddhist Hell's Angels. They were joined on Thursday by a group of plein air artists forming impressions of the scene on their easels. Other supporters came to the site to share the experience.

Dierdre Oppings, one of the artists, noted that, "If the scene is not recorded in revolutionary art, then it didn't really happen." She waved her "spirit fingers" in solidarity. "Usually, I spend my time painting on my Bambi meets Godzilla series," she said. "It is not art, but it pays the bills. Today is about art."

June Cleaver arrived to engage the gathering as a psychic facilitator. She gave a speech that focused on the noble sacrifice and martyrdom of Bud Cutler. She roused the crowd with bold statements on his creative genius, neurotic self-reliance, and obsessive insanity that somehow makes sense in a world where water theft is legal and fish have lawyers.

She mentioned his goal to protect the Eel. Then she yelled, "Now that he is gone, what are we going to do about it? What are we going to do!?... I say Conga Line for freedom, CONGA LINE FOR FREEDOM!"

Provocateurs seeded in the audience started chanting, "Conga, Conga" and someone began playing bongos. Slowly people got the beat and converged in a long winding conga line up to the ridge south of the tunnel entrance.

Meanwhile a vast militia funded by the Vineyard Association. of Sonoma with start-up funding from Disney Entertainment motored north to Mendocino. They rode a phalanx of golf carts and lawnmowers and carried golf bags in a bid for moral and financial support from the golfers in Sonoma County. The golf cart troops streamed colorfully printed flags behind them, marked with Disney lyrics like "Let it Flow" and "Once Upon a Stream."

As the mercenaries arrived at the site from the south, they were confronted by June Cleaver, staring down at them with steely eyes from the crest of the ridge. She was flanked by Bam Bam Ram and Bruce Anderson in front of a motley crew of rugged Jeffersonians and ragged tree-sitters in ghillie suits.

The Jefferson forces were wielding posters of Bud Cutler labeled "Peace Warrior," and "This Shit Don't Run," along with several posters of a cow with a thought-bubble saying "Blow Me."

It was a breezy day so when Ms. Cleaver yelled "Fire," they lit bales of shake in specially-vented 55-gallon steel barrels. The cloud of pot smoke wafted down over the golf carts.

In an audio pincer attack, Bam Bam Ram led a choir of Hell's Angels in a slow-building, deep-toned chant, in harmony with the roar of their bikes.

Then the sheriff stepped in front of the bikers for a tenor solo. He tooted the melody as he danced, grunted, and stooped in rhythm, grimacing.

Whip was standing next to your intrepid reporter and made a low sweeping gesture with his bandaged hand toward the performers. "The sounds of revolution," he said. "I was in San Francisco during the late sixties, so I've heard it before."

Down the hill, the mercenaries, who had been paid in boxes of wine and 5-pound tins of Costco mixed nuts, lifted the boxes high from their golf bags and thumbed the valves to splash wine into their open mouths to get courage up for the battle.

Then a bank of Cutler's Squirrel Cannon® artillery started firing from the Jefferson side behind some trees on the ridge. "Fwump, fwump, fwump" went the barrage. The artillery crew could be seen pumping furiously on the air banks while others were loading para-squirrels through the breach doors with welding gloves.

The guy conducting the artillery from high in a tree was Forrest Byrne. He was signaling frantic target corrections with elaborate gestures and chirping.

His timing of the cannon fire syncopated with the Choir of Angels and their throbbing Harleys. The music started sounding like the opening of 2001: A Space Odessey, with a tenor line like a tweety horn.

The first squirrels were tracer rounds made with stuffed toy animals in parachutes that wafted down from high above. Then they went live. Squirrel Team Six® shot from the cannons and swooped down low and fast with their little limbs spread in glide position, while their flight suits sparkled in the sun.

At first the mercenaries yelled out "Incoming, Incoming!" and raced around stomping on stuffed squirrels with their new golf cleats, their eyes aloft at the slowly settling parachutes.

When the live rounds started coming in, the startled mercenaries raced to protect their carts. But it was too late, by then the squirrels were landing on target and immediately raided the golf bags. "AAAArghhh," screamed one of the golf crew "they got my nuts."

Meanwhile, a few miles south of the other end of the tunnel, a caravan of trucks was barreling up the road trailing a cloud of dust. The lead truck was driven by Security God. Riding shotgun was Charles Osgood. Several camera drones from Disney were recording the charge, flying above, and circling about.

As the trucks came around a curve leading to the tunnel's mouth on a road section cut into the steep-sided canyon they were blocked by a sheriff's deputy squad car. Standing on the road in front of the car stood Deputy Buzz Mackey with a nonchalant smile and one hand raised to stop the caravan.

The trucks stopped and Dr. Osgood stepped out to confront the deputy.

Deputy Mackay said, "This road is closed by order of the sheriff. Please back your vehicles out of here."

Dr. Osgood clained, "We have permission from PG&E to access this road to repair the diversion tunnel. It's their road and their tunnel. You can't close it without a court order."

Mackay replied, "Well then, instead I will impound your vehicles under California Code 3981. Your devices qualify as hydraulic mining equipment. It is illegal to use that equipment in or near a stream in the State of California."

At the wheel of the lead truck, Security God shouted out, "Get your damn police car off the road or I will push it off. I am coming through." He revved the big engine and clanged the truck into gear.

Dr. Osgood scuttled off to the side, but Buzz Mackay stood his ground.

The truck roared, the gears shrieked, the huge engine shuddered, and then quit.

Security God started up again. The truck spit a cloud of exhaust, rumbled, clanged into gear, screeched, grumbled, and quit again.

Security God slammed open the door and looked back. Standing beside the back wheels were two more deputies having climbed up from below the road. They had big red clamps locked on the wheels, immobilizing the truck.

Buzz then said calmly, "Oh no you don't."

Meanwhile, in the battle back at the other end of the tunnel, a swarm of mercenaries had succeeded in remounting some of the golf carts by kicking off the golf bags filled with hungry squirrels. A large brigade of mounted homeless mercenaries then advanced up the hill at the smaller force of patriotic defenders.

Just then Russell Brand and I drove a herd of incontinent cows out of the woods and onto the upper portion of the slope.

The Jeffersonian forces started yelling down to warn the mercenaries, "Watch out, they might be loaded." Fortunately, the cows simply unloaded, together, sending a roaring flood of cow diarrhea downhill.

Just then the cannons let go another barrage. A few cows started nervously from the noise. One took off trotting. Then the whole herd accelerated after him, running down the hill making a rising thunder.

Russell stood in his stirrups and shouted "Watch out, it's a STAMPEDE!"

At first the herd thundered through the plein air artist colony. Artists started running. Some grabbed their easels while others scattered as easels and paintings got splattered and shattered or trampled and gored.

I was on Aragorn. Reflexively I yelled, "GET UP GIRL." She bolted and we raced down the hill after the herd. My head was roaring through the wind and I had no thought except to stay on, cow diarrhea splashing up around me with each hoof strike.

Galloping down the hill one of my shoes came out of the stirrup. I tried to shove it back in as Aragorn raced downhill, but my shoe wouldn't go in. I looked down and saw the stirrup bouncing around wildly.

Then the stampede ran down into a steep gully raising a great cloud of dust. Aragorn leaped down alongside them as I leaned all the way back on her butt. My free leg was bouncing crazily until I pulled it up onto her withers.

I yanked at my saddle horn to lean back up, one leg bent in front of me. Then I shouted "WHOA" and pulled on the reins, but Aragorn rushed on. Some of the cattle were wildly slipping and tumbling in the flow around me.

We came up on the head of the herd so I leaned forward shouting and waving my hat. I spied Russell coming up on Rama. Together, our horses thundering along, we turned the herd from the gully onto the valley floor and they ran, slowing, into a field by the reservoir.

God's warriors, shocked by the spectacle, spilled off their carts, floundered, sputtered, and spit lying in cow shit. They tried to stand up, just to slip down again. After their narrow miss with being trampled, the intoxicated, confused, filthy brown, and odorous, but now enlightened mercenaries raised their hands in surrender.

In my relief with the slowing herd, I suddenly remembered my youthful bike practice. Feeling elated, I stood up on my one leg that was already poised on Aragorn's shoulders, extending my other leg back as I held the reins to either side in a standing swan pose. I could hear cheers from God's warriors and the entire Mendocino crew through the slowing shuffle of hooves.

After that display, the combative attitudes on both sides fled and we all went skinny dipping in the Van Arsdale reservoir, made much safer now by the blockage of the diversion.

Above it all, a nearly transparent, flickering vision of Dr. Tang floated on a low cloud, meditating on the scene while sitting in lotus position in an ethereal robe with a serene smile between tightly closed lips.

The last ones to the reservoir were the artists, who after trying to salvage their kit, were walking down the hill, bedraggled, with their heads bowed, lugging their broken tripods, and dragging the remains of their paintings in the dirt behind them.

Ms Cleaver, the victorious leader, interviewed after the battle, was asked how she came up with the winning strategy. She elaborated on the AVA article about secession. "Our past revolutionary history includes the battle that stopped the nuclear plant at Bodega Head where they launched colored balloons carrying notes celebrating future fallout from a plant meltdown. Even the Black Panther's revolutionary action in Oakland mostly involved sharing food and medical care, at least until the police started gunning them down. Our future history should build on all that peace.

"Unfortunately," she said, "Our past history links secession with violence. So, now we focus on dissolution instead. Maybe we can agree to disagree.

"It is always better to engage in free love and joyous partying than war. Isn't that obvious?"

After the battle, I relive those chaotic moments careening through a downhill maelstrom composed of cows, horses, people, golf carts, and flying squirrels, all lubricated in some seriously slippery shit. My head spins with the thought. Then at that moment our two forces joined, I remember feeling like time stopped, and started again.

I realize that my friends at Dune Beach were wrong. It is not who I can become that matters, it is who WE can become that makes us powerful.

A loving culture has formed among the wildly varied characters here in Mendocino. I wonder how this kind of diversity can allow the genuine trust, acceptance, and joy I see and feel around me?

Meanwhile all the splashing just seems fun.

When it comes to skinny dipping in the reservoir, I join in. Anita is there too. When I see her, I think YOWZA and wade over.

"Well," she says "I can tell by your outfit that you have joined the local uprising."

It seems like I have gained some weight in her eyes. I wonder if it is my willingness to commit, being able to stay mounted when the bullshit went down, or the trick riding.

I say, "I got caught up in the moment."

Anita replies, "Yes, you have been showing off today... and you brought your horse." Then she stretches up and kisses me smack dab on the lips, my first real kiss.

I am stunned. But I think quickly enough to gently wrap my arms around her. I look in her eyes and ask "Why me?"

She says, "I'm not sure, but I want to find out."

Then stiffening, I say slyly, "Don't move. Did you see that snake in the water?"

Anita replies, wrapping her arms around my neck, "Nice try, Kit Carson." Then she looks, leans down, stabs one hand into the water after the snake, grabs, and pulls it out. She shakes it until it spits.

She says, "See the sucker-head on this thing? It's not a snake, It's a lamprey. You're just lucky it doesn't suck blood."

"Wow, nice grab," I say. "Maybe you can show me how you do that."

Anita replies, "Usually, you find them locked on to a rock. We used to sneak up on them slowly in the water. We would reach out to stroke them a couple of times to keep them calm, then yank them off."

Then she explains, "We hung out at the river in high school so I've had some practice. We always laughed when they spit."

"By the way," she continues, "I once brushed my hair with my hand after shaking a lamprey and found that

If you massage that spit in, it will curl your hair up tight."

I respond, "Really? Curl your hair? I take a moment feeling like I am channelling my Dad or maybe Godfrey. This seems like one of those opportunities. "Hmmm, maybe we can make some money with that in a self-care product line. If the curls are tight, we could call our hair curling lotion Afrodesiac®. That'll sell."

"That's not the hair I was talking about." She says, "And lampreys don't spit up much volume."

"No problem," I say enthusiastically, "We could dilute it with mucus from other animals. Then I say, "Sheep! sheep got curls!"

She looks at me a little funny then and laughs.

21

The Free State of Jefferson

Around us the wine boxes, soaked in the water, have come off and people are holding up the mylar bags of wine like bunches of grapes to serve each other. Others are laughing, singing, and splashing.

I ask Anita, "Have we finally created the State of Jefferson?"

She looks around, "Seeing how energetically we celebrate insanity around here, maybe we should call it the Asylum of Jefferson."

"Yes," I said, "It's crazy and yet wise and powerful. Jefferson: an asylum run by the inmates; it just makes sense."

Anita continues, "But we gotta get a new flag. That old State of Jefferson double cross flag is negative and boring."

After a minute I suggest, "How about Squirrel Team Six® gliding spangled across a blue sky like stars, above the pot smoke and dust of a stampede. That would make a flag!"

"Right," she says excited, "Then we put that in a circle that overlies the double cross to show how the future overcomes the past."

"I like it," I say. "By the way, are you hungry? I came prepared."

"Come to think of it, a little revolution can spark a woman's appetite. What do you got for me?"

"I liberated some mixed nuts and wine from one of the golf carts and I got a pickle."

"Yes, mixed nuts," she smiles looking around.

I finally know where I belong. After fleeing my depressing life and origins, I find my people here in the Free State of Jefferson.

We think differently up here, just like you. We figure that the best democracy is big enough to provide public services but small enough to share delusions. We don't plan to tell other groups how to live, and we expect a similar courtesy from them. Meanwhile we're gonna have a parade.

Later that day, Bruce Anderson reviews my first draft on the battle, then I see him at the café. He asks me whether Godfrey came to the rally. "I was hoping to sell more ads," he says.

"I saw him watching from a director's chair that he set up near his Delorean," I tell him. "He had a film crew. It looked like they were interviewing Landon Shore at the time."

"Meanwhile," I say, "If you sell him another ad, make sure to get cash. He's *all up high-pockety…* I mean rich. Sometimes they don't pay."

Bruce replies, *"High-pockety?* Are you speaking *Boontling* already? My, you *are* going to fit in."

I follow that with, "I noticed that you were up there with Ms. Cleaver. Given you were up there with the charismatic and military leaders, does that mean you are taking up the role of the bard, like Lenin? Or are you modelling Angela Davis, the Black Panther?"

Bruce says "I am thinking more along the lines of Abbie Hoffman from the Chicago Seven."

"By the way," he says then, "In your article, we should cut the reference to Forrest as a "guy in a tree."

"Why?" I ask.

"It's gender insensitive. We all grew up with Forrest, so we knew her when she was a woman. Now that he is a transvestite, we kind of let it happen."

I think about that for a moment. Should I tell Natasha, I ask myself? … No, I think, let her figure that one out herself.

Anxiety and fear of my ex-FBI agent tormentor strikes me hard at first, then after a moment, I smile, thinking about her as a new friend on a voyage of discovery, like me. The change will do her good. I feel touched.

I say to Bruce, "For years I thought I was someone else too. But now I am transformed." Thinking about who I have become, I say, "Maybe I am a kind of transvestite too."

Anita chimes in from bussing the next table, "No, he's not."

22

After the Future

The Second Patriotic Revolution of the State of Jefferson will generate a siren call to those that believe in freedom and community self-determination. Not just on the political right wing, but all of us. We can do this together if we focus on accepting all the kinky flavors of our local delusions.

In the future of the future, the complete rout of the water thieves at the Battle of Van Arsdale will never be challenged. The combined might of artists, Hell's Angels, tree sitters in ghillie suits, cow diarrhea, and the revolutionary press centered in Anderson Valley is revealed as a mighty force indeed.

Perhaps you feel that the idea of peaceful revolution as recounted in this future history is doomed. However, it may come down to whether you want to help with a peaceful transition to joyous but rational local cooperation or just watch as our mega-democracy crumbles around us in spitting and hateful division. And if you think secession will never work, then dissolution might put us onside with other secession movements around the country. Do you really want to be held back by wackos elsewhere? There are plenty of us right here to do the job.

The past history of the State of Jefferson and Eldridge Cleaver in this story are as true as the internet, including the references to Stan Delaplane's Pulitzer Prize and Eldridge Cleaver's career and innovative trousers. You can even watch the original NBC news film of the State of Jefferson parade in Yreka online and buy youthful blood transfusions to fight aging from a start-up in San Francisco. Henri Pujol actually performed as a flatulist at the Moulin Rouge for a few years. He was popular and unknowingly spawned a movement of sorts. Meanwhile, someone has already designed a wireless helmet that can be used for transcranial magnetic brain stimulation. Unfortunately, their version makes you look stupid. And the tragi-comedic history of the diversion and dam is based on a real geologic report made to the state. There is also a large Buddhist Temple outside of Ukiah although it is not led by a monk named Poon Tang with a PhD and a robe inspired by the Flying Nun.

Other partly true, more personal stories are woven in inaccurately as told me by residents of Mendocino County, including the ones involving Bill Graham, pot farmer washing machines, blowing shit up, and how to midwife a cow. Finally, some of these stories I experienced myself or are complete fantasies, although it is not clear which is which anymore.

You probably think I made up the part about the flying squirrels. However, there are plenty of nocturnal flying squirrels living high in the redwoods in Mendocino. They have bioluminescent bellies to help them land at night in neighboring trees. Unfortunately, they refused to work for peanuts, so we had to enlist some grey squirrel scabs for this story.

You may have noticed several inventions mentioned in this future history. I have done the easy part by making them up. They are mostly based on science, so we just need some good engineers to figure out how to put the tinkertoys together, then we can get rich. As usual though, while any fool can make this shit up, it will take a genius to market it… And, by the way, you're welcome.

Meanwhile the best invention of all was an accident. Those trampled paintings from the stampede ended up in an auction in a vacant building in downtown Willits hosted by Dierdre Oppings, the new Mendocino Art Commissioner. They got attention when some were bid up into the thousands as a record of the revolution. This started an artistic movement that spread worldwide and is now a key element of the migration to Pamplona for the running of the bulls. Artists, some affecting stubbly goatees, sloppy berets with glasses, and long extended holders for their vape pens, rent the rooms above the run so they can throw their paintings down into the fray, doubling their prices by completely ruining whatever the paintings were to begin with. It takes serious mental fortitude to sacrifice your art like that. But if you are an artist that is still among the living, you need the money.

Meanwhile Dierdre sold the story rights on the Jefferson side of the revolution to Disney in return for the copyright on Bambi paintings. You can look for them in Willits.

Although the Anderson Valley Advertiser is celebrated here as the voice of revolution, it is also a useful guide to community events and a testament to the idea that the journalistic arts can flourish in small towns. All the names in this story have been changed to protect the guilty, except for the editor, who is now a committed dissolutionist since it is the only peaceful path to both anarchy and socialism.

Finally, this revolution occurs in the future so there is no point in pretending that it can't happen. It's the future.

Afterword

If you liked this, I am happy for you. You are clearly easily entertained, which is totally a good thing. If you didn't like this book then you are not reading this afterword and are probably working on your taxes for fun.

If you want more, I am writing. I have ten or fifteen epic adventure poems. One of these we made into a beautifully illustrated children's book. I am also working on other books. One is a children's book that describes the adventures of two kids on their way to making a beautiful world in a changing climate. Another one is titled "The Care and Feeding of Dads." That book is a bunch of short stories based loosely on the tales I told my kids so that they wouldn't have to go to sleep yet. That book will be perfect for the end of the day when you are tired and it gets hard to make stories up for kids. Luckily, I am a geologist, that's what we do.

www.ingramcontent.com/pod-product-compliance
Lightning Source LLC
Chambersburg PA
CBHW071323150726
47997CB00002B/590